SCATTERED IN HIDDEN PLACES

A Short Story Collection

DAVID EVANS

CONTENTS

Out there
in the distance,
on the horizon,
something unexpected
is rising…

GROUND DOWN

Hardly had Remi raised his coffee cup to meet his lips in preparation to sip his first cappuccino of the day, when Dreyfus's words caused him to stop abruptly, look over the rims of his black thick-framed glasses and meet Dreyfus's gaze with fixed-eye surprise.

"What?"

"Like I said. I want out."

Remi's cup travelled back in the direction from which it came, towards the black gold-edged table for two, finally resting in its original position in the saucer, froth still intact.

"I'm done. I'm bored. The business doesn't excite me anymore."

"Come on Dreyfus, you can't be serious. We've only just got going."

"I know, but no more for me. Now it's the same routine every day."

"But routine is great. That's why I love it."

"Yes, I know, that's you Remi: safe, predictable, secure. But that's not me. For me the fun is over. For me building the business was the exciting part, but that's done now. It's up and running and doing very well, but now that we're there, I feel there's no challenge. A bit like buying a dilapidated house. The joy and motivation are in the renovating but once everything is complete it's time to move on and find another project to start from scratch." As he spoke, he felt a slight pain in his upper arm causing him to rotate the joint around the shoulder.

"But you can do that with this, Dreyfus. We can expand. Set up a second coffee shop, and then another, and another."

"Yes, I've thought about that but it's the same thing; it's just repeating what we've done. I'm looking for something new now. I'd like to do something completely different," said Dreyfuss, eyes squeezing as the pain became more intense.

"Come on Dreyfus, surely an expansion is like your renovation. There's still loads to do."

"Remi, my mind is made up. You can take on another partner. I'm sure there'll be plenty of interested parties," said Dreyfus, clearing his throat and breaking into an irritating cough.

"Are you okay?" asked Remi, patiently waiting for the cough to subside.

"Yes, I'll be fine," he replied, repeatedly bending his arm at the elbow in attempts to relieve his discomfort.

"Look, why don't you take the weekend to think about it?"

"Okay, if that makes you feel better, but it won't make a difference Remi," replied Dreyfus, now breaking into a slight sweat. "Actually, I'm feeling a little nauseous, I think I'll get some fresh air."

"Yes, I think you should; you're not looking too good," said Remi, eyes narrowing. "I'll fetch you a glass of water."

Dreyfus stood up tentatively and made his way towards the exit, delicately twisting and turning to edge through the narrow spaces separating the black gold-edged chairs, a shortness of breath creeping in as he stumbled through the doors and emerged into the open air. Remi ordered the water from the counter, and as he turned around, he caught a glimpse of two men hastily leaving their seats and heading outside. He immediately raced towards the commotion, himself now weaving through the narrow spaces guessing this was related to Dreyfus. As he pushed through the glass doors, he could see his partner lying spreadeagled on the pavement, the two men kneeling beside him, one making a call on his phone. Remi knelt down and peered into Dreyfus's eyes. The ambulance was on its way, but it would be of no use. He was not moving. There was no sign of breathing or of any response to speech and touch. There was no doubt. Dreyfus was dead.

Dreyfus's death at forty had a profound effect on Remi: the idea that life can cease so abruptly and without warning. Remi himself was already half-way through life's expectancy. It had now dawned on him that perhaps Dreyfus was right. Maybe he should do something different. Do something more exciting. Perhaps establishing his business was the exciting bit and running it was the boring bit. What would he do? What would really excite him now? What might he regret he had never done when his time comes?

"I've been having a good think, Ava. Life is short. Look at Dreyfus. Gone at forty. We should do something exciting."

"Exciting? What are you talking about? What do you mean by exciting? This is exciting. Establishing this business has been exciting. You've now got it going well. It's what you've always wanted."

"I realise that, Ava. I agree. But maybe this is a wake-up call for us. Grab our opportunities while we can, while we

10

are young, fit and healthy. Take a fresh look at what we really want. We could sell the business, or just arrange for someone to run it in our absence. Whatever. Travel. See the world. We can do it as a family. Go off for two years. Live a different life. Rent the house. We would have enough money to sustain us for a year or even two."

"Come on Remi, this isn't like you. And what about when we come back? What are you going to do? We'll be broke."

"I don't know yet but that's something we could think about. If you're with me on this, we can talk more seriously about it, explore what's possible. Plan it properly."

"And what about the children? We'd have to take them out of school."

"We can home school them. That's not a problem. It's not against the law. In fact, it's becoming quite popular."

"It's a huge thing to do Remi; I'm not sure it will be fair on the kids. Interrupt their education. Away from their friends."

"Yes, but look at what they'll gain. They'll see the world. The great sights. They'll gain all that experience. All that knowledge. It'll be a better education."

"Remi, I'm not sure. It's too much. Too dramatic a change. I don't want to do it."

The conversation was certainly not going Remi's way. His wife was obviously not on board with his idea, and it soon evaporated into thin air.

He continued to run the coffee shop with a new partner on board, Niko Harris, who had injected a new energy into the business, suggesting improvements and better experiences for customers. And there was one thing he believed they should both do which none of them had done despite being in the coffee business.

"Remi, we should go and visit a coffee farm. We run a coffee business yet none of us has actually seen the process for ourselves. We've just relied on research and recommendations, which is fine, and everything is going well, but don't you think it would be complete and fulfilling to see the whole process for ourselves?"

"Yes, it's a great idea. Where have you got in mind?" asked Remi without hesitation.

"Colombia. That's where our coffee beans come from so let's get over there and see for ourselves. We could extend the visit and take in some of the sights at the same time."

"Colombia! Wow, that would be some trip."

"We could do a ten-day tour to give us enough time for a good adventure. There's the Cocora Valley, the beautiful hot springs of Santa Rosa de Cabal, the mountains of Los Nevados National Park. It'll be fantastic."

"I'll have to talk to Ava first. We'll have to make arrangements for the coffee shop in our absence but I'm sure she'll agree. Compared to the world trip I wanted to go on, this will be a drop in the ocean. I'm sure it'll be fine."

"Colombia? Remi are you sure? It's never bothered you before about not seeing the coffee bean process. People sell plastic toys from China, but they don't have to go and see how they are made."

"Ava, this isn't just about coffee. It's a compromise for me, isn't it? An opportunity is arising for me to do something different. To have some form of adventure, excitement, get it out of my system. Niko seems a sensible guy."

"I don't know Remi. I'll be worried."

"Come on Ava, it will be fine. Niko's right, we should see the coffee growing process for ourselves. Part of the philosophy."

"How will you do it? Do they do organised trips from this country? I'll feel more comfortable if you did it that way."

"I'm sure they do, though Niko is pretty independent and will probably organise it all himself. Look, honestly, it will be fine."

"When have you got in mind?"

"The best time is May, so we'll plan for that."

"Okay, if that's what you really want. I suppose it's a far cry from upping sticks with our whole family for two years."

"Of course it is."

Remi and Niko sat beside each other on the plane drinking beer and eating on-board meals. Niko had planned everything. The Colombian Coffee Triangle would be the focus of the visit, the region famous for producing most of the Colombian coffee. They would visit Pijao and meet local farmers and people involved at every stage of the process: picking, where the rain would have provided the perfect conditions for growing coffee cherries, only the red ones required; milling, where the husks are removed leaving the raw coffee beans; drying, where the coffee beans are laid out in the hot sun; parchment removal, revealing the green coffee beans; and finally the roasting, where the silver skin chaff falls off and the beans become browner and crack open like popcorn.

As they emerged into the open air after the fourteen-hour flight, they were greeted by a torrent of rain. Across the concourse, they could see a row of squat yellow vehicles lining up to collect their fares, each with four doors, curved rear bonnet, yellow mirrors, yellow door handles, and small wheels with multi-spoke hub caps. They scurried onwards, heads down, dragging their wheelie cases through the pelting rain, merciless to the two new arrivals.

"Hotel Habitel please."

Their stationary position in the downpour whilst negotiating the fare ensured a complete drenching. They finally slumped into the back seat, wet hair flat to the head, water streaming down their faces, clothes dripping profusely, forming pools of water on the rubber mats beneath their feet.

"Welcome to Bogota," uttered the driver, a tone of amusement detected in his voice.

They drove on in silence for about half an hour, initially along tree-lined roads before the gradual emergence of narrower streets and colourful buildings, predominantly blues, oranges and yellows forming a variety of geometrical shapes.

On arrival at the hotel, situated half-way up a sloping narrow street, they stood passively outside the taxi having passed the point of caring about being soaked. They paid the fare and ambled casually towards the hotel entrance, heads up defiantly as the deluge continued. A refreshing shower would wash the welcome woes away and prepare them for the delights of a simple first night out. They would head straight to downtown La Candelaria to walk the narrow streets and see the architecture of the old churches and buildings. They would sample the local food and drink, especially a few glasses of aguardiente to put some fire in their bellies.

"Shit," screamed Niko from inside the bathroom.

"What's happened?" Remi called out, hearing Niko's cry.

"Nicked myself with the bloody razor," shouted Niko. "Won't stop bleeding."

"Stick some tissue over it!" yelled Remi.

A minute later Niko emerged from the bathroom, white tissue stuck to his cheek revealing bloody evidence of the razor blade's capability.

"Very nice Niko. Keep it on. It suits you."

"Come on. Let's get on with it. I can't wait to get out there," said Niko holding the tissue in place with his forefinger.

"I'm ready," replied Remi, having showered and dressed first.

As they arrived at reception, Remi noticed a solitary sombrero hanging on a coat rack.

"This looks great," said Remi as he grabbed hold of the hat to try it on."

"Put it down Remi. It's not yours."

"No, you can have it," interjected the receptionist. It's been there for ages, left by a guest."

"Are you sure?"

"Yes, no problem."

Remi placed the sombrero on his head.

"What do you think Niko?" asked Remi, as he posed in

the broad-brimmed hat, predominantly red, with yellow, blue and white stripes encircling the distinctive high pointed crown.

"You can't be serious. You look like a tourist."

"I am a tourist. Come on let's go. The cab is here."

The historic neighbourhood of La Candelaria likened itself to the 'Old City' in many major capitals. They were fascinated by the art deco styles, adored the narrow cobblestone streets, and admired the vivid street-art of Colombia depicting legends from the pre-Colombian era, particularly being captivated by two volcanoes resembling two figures, one lying in a sleeping position and the other kneeling at its side. After an hour, with light fading and weary from the travelling and walk, it was time for the much-anticipated food and drink: enticing empanadas and alluring aguardiente. Definitely lots of aguardiente.

"Well, we made it Niko. A bit of a long-haul journey but here we are," said Remi, raising his glass of the famous liquor.

"Yes, it's great to be here. Cheers," replied Niko, raising his own glass, and reaching across the table to meet Remi's with a gentle clink signalling the beginning of their much-awaited adventure. The two men ordered their food and chatted away excitedly, the conversation becoming deeper as the alcohol took effect, both men loosening up, discussing life, their ambitions, their hopes, and their dreams.

"So, is this going to be enough adventure for you Remi? It's a far cry from a round-the-world trip with your family."

"Well, it's a start. Maybe Ava's right. Uprooting the

family for a couple of years was a step too far. No, this will do for now. Maybe the next step will be a more adventurous family holiday. An African Safari or maybe the Canadian Rockies. I'm sure Ava will run with that. Something a bit more than lying on a beach."

"So, this new take on life is all due to Dreyfus's death?"

"Yep. He was so young. And seeing him die right in front of me, you just realise that life is so short. Anything can happen. You suddenly think about what you really want in life. Of course, family is important, work can be exciting in its own way, but there has to be some other form of adrenalin rush. Some true excitement within life surely, where you actually feel physical sensations in your body. Yes, for sure, Dreyfus's death changed my outlook completely." Remi tipped his head back and poured the last drops of his third glass of liquor down his throat. "What about yourself? I don't really know that much about you, other than your business background and successes. All I know is you are 'Mr Single', a bachelor man with the world at his feet. Am I right?"

"Spot on. I love it. You can do what you like when you like. Money is important of course and I've got plenty of that."

"No desire to settle down yet then?"

"No, I'm happy as I am."

"So, what does it for you? What's your idea of excitement?" asked Remi.

"Well, I'm not craving the big adventure like you. I get it. You are in your routines, working, raising your family and you need that big vacation, the dramatic change of scenery, a completely contrasting way of life for a short period of time, something to look froward to, a change

17

from the everyday. But for me it's different. My excitement comes *from* the day to day. Being free. To do what I like when I like. No accountability. Nights out, friends, dinners, women, theatre and yes, travel, regular weekends away. Family life's not for me. I'd be tied down, too much responsibility."

"So, no big ambition then? No ultimate goal in life? No kids?"

"Nope. And definitely, no kids," said Niko, a slight redness flushing in his cheeks.

Finally staggering out of the restaurant, darkness now predominant, and eager to get back to the hotel, Niko raised his hand at the first taxi that came into view.

"Not sure that's a yellow cab, Niko. You know what they said. Stick to the reputable taxi drivers."

"Remi, it's fine. It'll be completely safe. They also said that those days are gone. That's how it used to be. Times have changed."

The taxi pulled up alongside the men.

"Bogota please. The Habitel Hotel," said Niko.

"No problem. Get in Sir," said the driver, in kind, friendly tones.

Remi and Niko climbed into the back and pulled their seat belts across their chests. The car drove off. After a few turns down several streets, it suddenly pulled over, two men appearing each side of the rear passenger doors. Each door was opened instantly, and the two men stood there, knives in hands, pointing directly at Remi and Niko.

"You," to Niko, "move over," ordered the black-bearded one, thick eyebrows pointing down at the centre, eyes narrowing, piercing.

Niko, without hesitation, obeyed the man's command

and shuffled over to the middle. The thug climbed in beside him. His accomplice, equally unpleasant looking, large mouth and rotting teeth dominating a long narrow face, slammed the other rear door shut and climbed into the front. The car sped off, knives visible, one pointing directly at Niko.

"Now gentlemen. Firstly phones." He held out his hand. Niko and Remi handed them over. There was no way they were going to risk pretending they didn't have any.

"We're going to a cash point," said black-beard man.

"You will get out one at a time and withdraw as much cash as you can," he ordered, wielding the knife in front of Niko's face.

"No worries, we'll do as you say," said Niko, voice quavering, eyes fixed on the blade.

"No problem," added Remi.

"Good. Glad to hear you know what's good for you."

Remi could feel the physical changes taking over his body - chest tightening, rapid breathing, heart pounding, stomach churning, goosebumps. Niko was also no longer in control of his bodily functions, his mouth becoming increasingly dry as the saliva ceased to exist. His brain, assessing the danger further as programmed to do, was telling him to flee, remove himself from danger. But this was not possible, not with this hoodlum by his side, his accomplice in the front seat and the driver in control of the door locks.

Within three minutes the car pulled over, an ATM light visible on the adjacent wall. Remi was first to be ordered out. As he approached the cash machine to withdraw the money, he thought about running. But what if they caught him? They would be aggravated. Would they kill him? Would they drive somewhere and kill them both? Stab them to death. He thought about the fact that this could be it. This could be the end of the road. The very end of life. In the most gruesome way. He thought of his family, his wife, his children. All he wanted at this moment in time was to be back in the comfort of his own home, within the love of the family, within the safety of the mundane, routine day to day life of running his business. Oh, how much he now wanted to simply serve a coffee to a customer. Flat white sir, certainly sir. Anything else? A croissant? Certainly sir. Take a seat and I'll bring it to you. At the same time, he thought about the horror of death. About the pain he may face. The actual agony of being stabbed, or being punched in the face, or the stomach. Oh my God. No. Please. No. In films people seem to fight on forever unhurt, the consequences and aftermath of injury never given attention. But in real life, one punch in the stomach can land you in hospital. One punch to the jaw can put you in the dentist's chair for weeks. How could they have been so naïve as to have got into this taxi in the first place?

He withdrew three hundred pounds worth of Colombian pesos, the maximum he could withdraw, and returned reluctantly to the car. Niko was next. The bastards, he thought. How dare they invade my life in this way. As he stood to enter his pin, he quickly thought about how he could get out of this situation. He could run; he was fast, well he used to be fast. Not anymore, more likely he would stumble and fall over. Anyway, this would leave Remi alone, exposed to these marauding brigands. Would they really use the knives? Or is it all a bluff? They are petty thieves, he was sure, not killers. All they want is the money. He would reason with them when he got back inside the car. There was nothing else he could do. He handed the money over.

"That's as much as I can withdraw, the same as my friend. Now can you let us go please?"

"In good time. We'll find a place to dump you first."

"Come on guys, just let us out. You've got our cash."

"Shut your mouth," snarled rotting teeth man, his knife suddenly raised and pointing towards Niko's throat.

The car drove on, the lights of La Candelaria disappearing behind them. They'd lost track of time. They could have been travelling for half an hour, two hours. The car stopped. Niko and Remi were escorted out of the back seat by knifepoint. A glimmer of light from the moon above helped provide just enough illumination to reveal some sort of building in which they were to be abandoned. They were told not to move, or they would face the consequences. The car drove away, the sound of the engine gradually becoming fainter as it disappeared into the distance.

It was complete darkness in the building. Both men heeded their kidnappers' words and remained where they were, too afraid to go outside. Sleep seemed impossible, but as time went on each one drifted off for a few minutes intermittently. There was nothing they could do until dawn. As daylight began to emerge through the cracked and broken windows, Niko opened his eyes to be confronted by a broad triangular head with a pair of piercing black eyes set in a continuous stare towards him, fork tongue flicking in and out of its mouth, sensing its prey, ready to strike.

21

"Jesus Christ," he whispered to himself, instantly realising not to yell out. "Remi, Remi. Look."

Remi turned his attention towards Niko and froze at the vile vision before him. He could just make out a gold and black elongated shape, about six feet, a scaly X pattern along its length, its head and upper body raised, pointing directly at Niko.

"Niko, don't move," whispered Remi.

Niko couldn't move if he wanted to. He was motionless with fear.

"What shall I do Remi?"

"Don't provoke it. Stay calm. Keep still. Maybe it will back off and go away."

Both men were terrified. They were experiencing their second bout of extreme horror in hours, their bodies barely recovering from the previous release of cortisol and adrenalin, blood flooding away from their hearts and into their limbs preparing them for flight. But right now, that would probably be the last thing they should be doing, stillness and a calm demeanour being the best course of action. Lying beside Niko on the ground was a half metre length of wood, just one of a number scattered around the building floor.

"There's a stick right by my foot. Shall I try and get it?" whispered Niko, lips hardly moving.

"No, don't move a single muscle."

Ignoring Remi's instruction, Niko slowly bent his knees to lower his body towards the ground, his aim being to edge his fingers closer to the stick.

"Niko, what are you doing?" whispered Remi through gritted teeth. "Stop."

Niko continued to bend his knees, in slow motion, eyes

fixed on the snake, head completely still, fingers now touching the stick. The snake stared back, its lengthy body slowly twisting and turning. Remi's eyes were wide open in fear. There was nothing he could do now; Niko was going to make the first move. He lowered himself a little further until he knew he could grasp the stick. He would need to be quick, thrust it towards the snake, enough to strike it or at least to distract it from its target. His mind was ready to stimulate his body into action when the snake lurched forwards at lightning speed, sinking its fangs into Niko's hand. Niko's instant reaction in panic and pain was to swiftly withdraw his hand, the snake momentarily hanging on as its fangs sank deeper into the skin before suddenly dropping to the ground. Remi immediately picked up the stick and madly and wildly beat away at the snake with all his energy, arms flailing in every direction, causing it to retreat and slither off into the shadows and hopefully out of the building. Niko was slumped on the floor holding one hand with the other, examining the damage, his heart racing and mouth dry. Two puncture marks were clearly visible, the hand now red, swollen, and painful.

"Christ Remi, I've been bitten."

Remi moved towards Niko to inspect the wound.

"Bloody hell Niko."

"What if it's poisonous?" gasped Niko, leaning up against the wall, now breathing very rapidly from the combination of shock and reaction from the venom.

"Niko, listen, take deep breaths, try to calm down."

Niko inhaled deeply and slowly trying to stabilise and bring his heart rate down.

"Good, that's good. Keep going. That's it. Deep breaths."

Niko's heart however, continued to pound at a rapid pace, the deep breathing not making much difference. Beads of perspiration poured down his face.

"My mouth feels weird Remi. It's gone numb and everything seems blurred."

"Shit. Niko, try and keep calm."

The bottom line was that Remi didn't know what to do. The venom was already taking effect. There was no way of getting any medical attention. He was just a spectator, watching his colleague suffer and worsen as the venom speedily made its way through Niko's body. He could only wait, comfort, reassure, and hope that the bite would not be fatal. As these thoughts crossed his mind, Niko began to shake uncontrollably, his body rigid one moment and jerky the next. Raising his hand to his throat, now swollen as his breathing tubes became restricted, he managed to whisper a few words.

"Remi…go…get help. There's nothing you can do…"

"No Niko. I can't leave you."

"Go…it's the only way. Go."

Remi thought hard. It was the only way. The best thing he could do was to try and get help. How? Who? He didn't know, but he did know that Niko's best chance of survival was to leave him and get medical attention.

"Niko, I'm going to lie you down on your side." Remi gently lowered Niko onto his back and pulled him over into the recovery position, facing him downwards, slightly to the side supported by his bent limbs, and finally ensuring his head was tilted back to open the airways as much as possible.

"I'll be back. I promise."

Remi made his way out of the building, daylight now

revealing a vast expanse of grassy, sloping plains dotted with clumps of trees. Mountains loomed in the background. A dirt track led away from what was now clearly a derelict, deserted stone house. This was the obvious route to take. He set off without water or food, still dressed in his blue denim jeans and beige linen jacket. The hat had disappeared long ago. He walked on for what seemed like a couple of miles, the sun gradually rising. Surely, the dirt track would soon lead to a more substantial road surface. He became increasingly tired and sat down to rest, removing his jacket and placing it over his head, his thin spread of hair forming little protection from the sun's burning rays. Feeling more and more demoralised with no sign of the dirt track ending, he knew he had to call upon all his strength and reserve to push himself on.

Niko could already be dead, he thought. He believed he had let him down, thinking there must have been more he could have done to save him, some action he could have taken to prevent the snake from striking. It could easily have been him. It was just random that it happened to be Niko; they were side by side. The snake chose Niko; God chose him. Or had God chosen Niko? He then began to think whether all these events had really happened. Was he really in Colombia? He tried hard to believe that this was not reality, that it was some sort of dream. Yes, it's a dream. Come on, wake up. He's been in these sorts of dreams before, where you fight to get out of them, to wake up, and you do. Not this time. He must carry on. Get out of here. Get home to his family. Get up again in the morning to serve his customers. God, those villains could come back. It now dawned on him that he may not survive. His own selfish desire for adventure came to the forefront of his mind. Dreyfus's death was the starting point for taking him to thoughts of 'life is short' and that we must grab it while we can. This could now turn into his death. Those bastards. He could kill them. Yes, if they appeared right now, and he had the chance, he would kill them, no question. So, we do have it in us to kill if the circumstances present themselves, he thought. This is the point he had come to in his life. He had read so many cases where people have killed in self-defence and pondered over whether it was true that we all have it within ourselves to kill. Well, it was within him right now. This man, a simple coffee shop owner, whose whole aim each day was to provide his customers with a nice cup of coffee, and who simply just wanted to provide for his family and lead a good life, now had the thoughts to end the lives of other human beings. This meek and mild-mannered man was now a potential killer. If they do come back, I've got nothing to defend myself with. I might have the determination to fight, but I haven't got the strength, the power, the weapons. Remi felt helpless. He had gone through a continuum of feelings from anger, power, and vengeance to helplessness, weakness, and fear. To survive, he would have to choose which person he wished to be. Thoughts turned to his family and children. Images appeared in his mind: tucking Mia into bed, the duvet up to her chin, eyes adoringly looking up at him.

"Goodnight, Mia. Sleep tight, see you in the morning."

"Night night Daddy."

Then into Leo's room, sitting cross-legged on the floor engrossed in his Lego.

"Come on now Leo, into bed you go, there's a good boy."

"But Daddy, I'm nearly finished. Just a few more pieces to go."

"You can finish it in the morning Leo. Come on now, into bed."

Ava preparing the lunch boxes in the kitchen before their late dinner, just the two of them, a glass of wine and home cooked fish pie.

Remi rose from his seated position, the feeling of terror departing from his body. I am going to survive. I am going to get back to my family. I don't care what comes my way. Bring it on. Whatever it may be. Snakes. Kidnappers. Killers. Heat. Thirst. Hunger. I will beat them all. I will return to my family.

Niko was deteriorating. The venom had established itself in his body. He was becoming delirious, drifting in and out of consciousness, no longer having any awareness of the passage of time. Whilst he was still able to think straight, he thought of the irony of being in this position, struggling to breath, now realising that death could be upon him much sooner than he had anticipated. Sooner than the eighteen months he had been given to live before the cancer would kill him, though maybe this is better than the gradual deterioration of his body the disease will bring upon him, becoming helpless and dependent on people. His mind's eye switched to the events which had brought him to this moment in time: the bogus taxi, the gruesome abductors, the flashing blades, the sinuate snake, and the deadly puncture marks from its penetrating fangs. His thoughts blended into nothingness as he fell asleep.

Niko's visions recommenced in his dreams: initially, standing before the priest, ring in hand and about to place it on his beautiful bride's finger, unusually dressed in a black bridal dress adorned with dazzling golden stars, the action being interrupted by a sudden severe dryness in his throat, causing him to struggle to continue his wedding vows. To his right his best man, Remi, mouth drawn down, eyes staring intensely. Then, a hospital setting, more specifically the labour and delivery room, Niko witnessing the birth of his son, experiencing overwhelming feelings of joy and love, tears rolling down his cheeks, unpleasantly interrupted by a shortness of breath, his chest tightening as he prepares to take the baby into his arms for the first time. Then, the labour room becomes his childhood bedroom. He is hiding, curled up into a ball, terrified from the yelling and screaming of his parents from downstairs, wanting to yell out to them to stop, but prevented from doing so from the numbness in his mouth, fearful of the inevitable storm in his room, to be dragged out of the house by his drunken mother, "Come on, we're leaving!" only to return an hour later after walking the streets to his sleeping father spreadeagled on the settee, two deep wounds visible in his swollen left hand, and his mother would climb into bed and immediately fall asleep, and he would return to his bedroom and cry.

As Remi continued his hike along the dirt-track, he thought he could hear a distant explosion. He stopped and waited. Did he really hear it? It could not be a crack of thunder as the sky was cloudless. He listened carefully. There it was again, louder, more of a misfiring sound. He stood still for two minutes but heard nothing. Then, appearing around a bend in the distance, he could just make out a moving vehicle, a truck of some sort, and as it gradually came nearer, he could make out a broad silver grill reflecting the sunlight. The sound came again. This time a loud bang. It was now obvious that these explosive sounds were caused by the truck's exhaust backfiring. However, Remi realised that the road the truck was travelling along was not the road he was on. Unless he moved fast the truck would cross by him at the distant junction. But then again, it could be those guys coming back. But it may not. He had to take the gamble. One way or the other there was a great chance of him dying anyway. He ran as fast as he could, calling upon all his reserves to catch the truck at the right time, frantically waving his arms in the air to flag it down. He could just make out a solitary figure behind the wheel. At first it looked like the truck didn't intend to stop, but when almost immediately upon him, the driver slammed on the breaks accompanied by another loud crack. The truck, its dark brown paintwork evident in places but mostly hidden by a murky covering of dust, came to an abrupt stop. Remi raced to the driver's window, already wound down.

"Thank God! Thanks for stopping."

"Esta bien," replied the man. "Cuál es el problema?"

"Ah, habla usted Ingles?

"Ah, Si."

"My friend has been bitten by a snake. Back down that track. He may already be dead. I don't know. Can we go there? Rescue him? Now!"

"Si, of course. Get in."

Remi ran round to the other side of the truck, wrenched open the door and climbed up into the cabin. The driver released the handbrake, slammed down his foot on the accelerator and sped off, once again a series of cracks and bangs accompanying the process.

Remi explained what had happened.

"Esos bastardos. There's been a spate of all that stuff lately. Thought we'd got rid of that sort of thing, pero todavia continua."

"Just keep going. I've walked for ages, but it can't be far in the truck. You'll eventually come to an old stone house."

"Ah, si, I know it. Been deserted for years."

They sped on and ultimately the stone house came into view. Remi's heart raced as he anticipated what may come next. He swiftly opened the door immediately the truck stopped, jumped out of the cab, and ran towards the house. Niko was there, in the same position, curled up on his side. Motionless. Remi ran over to him, closely followed by the driver, knelt down on both knees and peered closely into Niko's ashen face. He held his cheek close to Niko's mouth. There was a faint sign of breathing. Yes definitely. He was alive. But they had to move fast. He still may not survive.

"Come on, let's get him in the truck. Pronto!" instructed Remi.

They both stumbled away as they carried Niko by the shoulders and legs and carefully lifted him into the cabin. Remi would sit with him and support him.

"How far is the hospital?"

"Un largo camino. But I know a doctor on the way. Avisare por radio"

***

There was no doubt that Remi had been deeply scarred by his experience: sleepless nights, reliving the horror in his dreams, self-blame - was there more he could have done? Or something different he should have done? Guilt at being the survivor. He even refurbished the coffee shop, replacing the sophisticated gold and black seating with a simple dark blue, rejecting a bright coloured pattern theme as this only took him back to his Colombian nightmare. Worst of all, due to his irritability, he was struggling with his relationships within his family, frequently arguing with Ava and being short tempered with the children. Gradually, over time, Remi began to come to terms with his experience. Family life improved and normality returned.

Carrying a cappuccino over to one of his customers, Remi was distracted by a huge explosive sound from outside, accompanied by an ear-deafening roar. He immediately swung his body round to peer out of the window, spilling the coffee as he did so, causing the saucer to flood and the frothy liquid to overflow onto the floor. A yellow, souped-up, Audi TT with oversized multi-spoked alloy wheels and customised rear spoiler could be seen revving its engine wildly and impatiently at the red light, intermittent popping and backfiring sounds contributing to the unpleasant din. It seemed to go on for an eternity until at last, the lights changed to green, and the car sped off with a loud crack.

Remi, freeing himself from his frozen position and momentary trance-like state, apologised to the customer and returned to the counter to make a fresh coffee, removing his phone from his back pocket as he did so. After scrolling through his albums, he found the photograph he was looking for, forwarded by Ava, the only photo he had sent whilst beginning the trip, a selfie of himself and Niko, arms wrapped around each other's shoulders, huge grins on their faces, each holding a glass of aguardiente raised towards the camera.

TÖLTÖTT KÁPOSZTA

He left Budapest on the ten thirty train to Pekas, fortunate enough to have found a table seat where he could set up his laptop, position his coffee, and eat his refreshments in a civilised manner, the only disadvantage being the fact that it was located next to the buffet carriage. The constant opening and closing of the sliding doors would annoy him, but he was prepared to tolerate this, prioritising space and comfort as key requirements for a satisfying journey. It was a state-of-the-art train, free from worn faded fabric dulled and dirtied by thousands of passengers over decades of use, but not perfect, the seats being uncomfortably hard for travelling long distances. The large, panoramic window provided the essential barrier between the comforting warmth of the carriage and the icy winter air outside. Although the cloudless sky was beautifully blue, and the sun shone with a summer's smile, the bare trees reminded him that this was winter: January darkness, abbreviated days, and for Tomas Luca, an abbreviated marriage. Not of his own choosing. Seventeen years of, in his mind, dedication, loyalty and togetherness. He had never thought there was an issue. That his wife wasn't happy. That she wasn't fulfilled. There were no children, but this, he believed, was what kept them together, what made them such a good team. No distractions.

The divorce officially brought an end to the life to which he had become accustomed – a union - sharing, caring, someone to come home to, someone to talk to, someone to share his bed. Now he was filled with despair, not just at the misery of facing the years ahead without

Zsofia, but at having to face the inevitable financial consequences of a marriage breakdown, forcing him back to where his life began, where the cost of living would be less expensive, a place to which he swore he would never return.

His memories of small-town life in Pekas had now manifested themselves in the forefront of his mind. They weren't fond memories: bullied in the parks, chased down streets, beaten in the dance halls. This type of recreation for youths was common-place, particularly late at night in Kossuth Street where just before midnight, it would be time for the weekly fight between the Torok and Cerna brothers – headlocks, fists, boots. Gang rivalry extended into Sunday morning football, pitches becoming battlefields. He couldn't escape these undesirable types. There would always be someone in the bar, or park, or café, people he had seen in their worst light, marring his enjoyment of the present, causing him a sense of unease, even in sedate surroundings: the river on a sunny summer's day, Saturday night cinema, swimming at the local pool. There was never any anonymity. Everybody knew everybody. But there was one thing very appealing about Pekas at this precise moment in his life: it offered financial security. As the only surviving member of the family, he had inherited a property and decided he would take on the house regardless of its condition. No point in selling it; the amount would hardly pay a deposit in Budapest. Better to take advantage of a wonderful opportunity. This house meant no mortgage. What he remembered of his aunt was that she approached matters of cleanliness and tidiness in a meticulous manner and there was no way she would ever allow her home to decline into some sort of slum. The overnight stay, he was sure, would confirm his decision to keep the property, which subsequently, would provide him with a new start and the reward of financial freedom. Within his current circumstances, out of the blue, out of the melee of uncertainty and despair from the split with Zsofia, he had been presented with a solution to his anticipated reduction in disposable income. This is all that mattered to him now. He could continue his work as an accountant on-line from home. Of course, it was a choice, and for Tomas Luca the return to Pekas and the advantages it offered far outweighed the worrying prospect of remaining in the capital with high rents, meagre spending money and continued pressure to work for a sustainable salary. Right now, it offered a better quality of life.

After travelling for an hour, longer than expected, the train stopped at Vecsela, the electronic seat indicator informing him that he would have company for the remaining duration of the journey. Several passengers appeared through the sliding doors, none of them taking a seat at his table, until the last person to board glanced down the carriage, and, not seeing anywhere else to sit, politely asked Tomas if the seat opposite was vacant.

"Seems to be," replied Tomas.

"Thank you," the man replied, placing his newspaper on the table, and removing his navy-blue cashmere coat.

"I'll certainly be claiming a refund."

"Sorry?" said Tomas, quizzically.

"The trains. I was meant to be on the previous one, which was cancelled, and now this one is late."

Tomas smiled and immediately returned his attention to his laptop. The train eased into motion, gaining speed, silently and effortlessly. Tomas's thoughts turned to his wife - his ex-wife. He had become boring, she had said. She wanted more social interaction, more contact with other couples: drinks, restaurants, dinner parties, holidays. He wanted just the two of them. He had tried at first but was averse to her idea of social contact, which mainly involved *her* friends, or work colleagues who would bring their husbands and wives over to dinner, but he found too often that he had nothing in common with these people.

"Oh, by the way, I'm Keleman."

Keleman was in his mid-forties, with a smooth complexion for his age, a generous head of greying hair, and clear framed glasses providing him with an appearance of a studious intellectual.

"Going to Pekas?" he asked.

"Yes," Tomas nodded, returning his attention to his work, not particularly wishing to engage in conversation.

The train travelled on through the countryside, Tomas at his laptop and Keleman scrolling on his phone, the sliding doors opening and closing repeatedly. Through the panoramic window a hint of cloud could be seen in the distance, scarring the vast expanse of blue. During this period, both men would glance up at each other, politely smile, and return to their convenient distractions. For Tomas, however, a slight feeling of uneasiness began to emerge in his mind. Keleman's face revealed a familiarity. In his mind's eye, he removed Keleman's glasses, shaved his hair to a number one and imagined what he looked like as a teenager: the deep-set glaring eyes, the dimples each side of his mouth, the prominent nose:
Dev.

I'm sure it's him, he thought. The gang leader, full of

bravado when backed up by his distasteful followers. That time at the snooker hall. Winner stays on. Not Dev. Protest, and the result will be a black eye from the butt end of the cue. Tomas could personally vouch for that. Everywhere Dev went there was trouble. It was him, or his gang, or others like them, who would appear at Tomas's haunts. He was popular with the girls though - they did love a bad boy. And, perhaps not in keeping with the traits of a bully, from what he could recall, Dev was tremendously successful at school.

His mind switched back to Zsofia. Was I really that boring? he thought, recalling Zsofia's first declaration of intent that she wanted to end the marriage. He certainly never saw the affair coming. Though it was never really about the affair, she had tried to explain. That was just the catalyst that would bring everything to a head. Zsofia had tasted something different, something more exciting, in stark contrast to her humdrum life with Tomas, a life that had become predictable, wearisome, and dull.

Meanwhile the train ploughed on, the weather looking ominous, grey clouds the dominant feature, sliding doors increasingly annoying. The ten-twenty from Mikolisk thundered past in the opposite direction, causing Tomas to jolt and knock over his coffee, fortunately lidded, so as not to cause too much of a spillage, milky brown liquid now trickling towards Keleman's newspaper. Tomas quickly grabbed a tissue. "Just made it."

Keleman had already raised his newspaper off the table.

"No worries," replied Keleman. "It's always a shock when those trains suddenly shoot by. Let me buy you another one."

"No honestly, it's fine. I'd practically finished it anyway.

Thanks all the same."

"A pleasure," replied Keleman.

"By the way, your face looks familiar. Do I know you?" asked Keleman.

Tomas had already felt apprehensive about whether to seek confirmation as to whether this was indeed Dev. He felt obliged to reveal his identity.

"Yes, I think you do. Tomas Luca. We were at school together."

"Yes, I can see you now. I just needed the name. Do you recognise me?"

"I had just been thinking about it. Yes. Keleman Deveny. Dev."

"Well, it's been years. Good to see you."

"Good to see you too," replied Tomas, his gentle smile admirably hiding his distortion of the truth.

The two men became immersed in inevitable reminiscences about the old days: school life, memorable venues, ultimate career paths. Initially, Tomas felt aggrieved that he now had to sit with this person, whom he remembered only as a thug and a bully, in polite conversation for what would be the remainder of the journey, but Tomas discovered what appeared to be a very different Keleman Deveny to the one he knew in those days. He had also been glad to escape Pekas. His outstanding academic ability had become the key to a new future, enabling him to achieve his ambition to study law. He was no stranger to the courts, as Tomas knew only too well, having been in trouble so frequently in his teens: fighting, stealing, vandalism.

"The irony was that this exposure to the legal system inspired me to find out more about the law," said

Keleman. "I wanted to make amends. Do good. Help people. I went to university, glad to be free from familiarity, and reminders of my father's departure when I was thirteen, apparently to seek work, but I never saw him again."

"So, what's the purpose of today's journey?" asked Tomas. "I assume you are going to Pekas."

"Yes, I ensure I make a couple of trips a year to visit family and friends. It's very different now, seeing the town from a new perspective. The museum, the art gallery, the concert hall. We didn't bother with those places in those days."

"No, you're right. They were for the oldies," said Tomas convincingly, recalling in his mind how much he loved expanding his knowledge of natural history in his spare time.

"Now we can appreciate the diversity of the neighbourhood, and of course afford the finer things the town offers – the best restaurants, the Zsinko Hotel, the relaxing escapism of the local mineral spa."

The conversation continued, Keleman revealing additional evidence of a successful transition from feral teen to mature adult: a well-respected barrister, happily married, two children both on track to be equally successful in their careers, living in an affluent area of Budapest and involved with charity work for The Hungarian National Heart Foundation following the death of his mother. Keleman even admitted recollection of his awful behaviour towards Tomas recalling in detail his aggressive and violent nature, putting it down to anger at the departure of his father, and apologised. Tomas's immediate, involuntary reaction was to feel a hint of desire to relax in Dev's company, to open up and reveal his current woes and circumstances, in particular his concerns about returning to his home town, of course omitting the elements that referred to Dev's contribution, but memories of hate and dislike countered that initial response causing him to resist such an extreme reaction. This was the infamous Dev: bully, tormenter, undesirable nasty piece of work.

The countryside whizzed past as the train sped on towards the next stop approximately twenty minutes away, intermittent high pitched screeching sounds causing Tomas to screw up his eyes and put his hands over his ears.

"I'm going to get another coffee," said Tomas, needing an excuse to get away for a few minutes. "Would you like one?"

"No, not for me thanks."

"Okay. Back in a while."

Tomas shuffled across the vacant adjacent seat, towards the sliding doors awaiting his silent command, and disappeared into the buffet car. He ordered the coffee, deep in thought, as the bar steward prepared an Americano. He couldn't believe what was happening. Here he was, all these years later, politely chatting away with one of the very people who put him off from returning to his home town in the first place, and indeed, why he had stayed away for so long. Was Dev telling the truth? Had he really reached the dizzy heights of a lawyer? Was this unsavory character now living a better life than him?

Tomas returned to his seat. The train gradually decreased its speed as it approached Eszterkolc. The conversation continued around the topic of the virtues of adult life in Pekas. Tomas, however, continued to feel tense in Dev's company. Relief came in the form of an announcement over the loudspeaker:

"Due to a technical fault, this train will not travel beyond the next station. Passengers are requested to disembark at Eszterkolc and await the next train; this will arrive in approximately fifty minutes. We apologise for any inconvenience this will cause to passengers."

Keleman was first to react. "I don't think I want to wait here for fifty minutes. I'll get a taxi. I'll be in Pekas before the train. Do you want to join me?"

"No thanks. I've still got some work to complete and want to get it done before we get there. I'm happy to wait." Tomas did not want to spend any more time with Keleman Deveny.

After a trip to the toilet and a sandwich in the station café, twenty minutes remained until the arrival of the fourteen-thirty-five. With no room under the sheltered area of the platform due to the extra number of passengers, Tomas had no option but to stand in the pouring rain, relieved to be separated from Dev but apprehensive more than ever with anticipation of life back in Pekas. Was this a big mistake?

The last hour of the journey saw Tomas deep in thought about what went wrong with his marriage. The bottom line was that Zsofia no longer wanted to be with him. She had found someone new. Her affair had been going on for a year. He couldn't believe that throughout this time he had never suspected anything. Life had been pretty much normal, Tomas working close to home in the offices of Orso Accounting and Zsofia commuting into Harkas, very different environments but they would always reunite at home for an evening dinner of cold meat, fruit and bread followed by television, apart from the occasions when she would need to work late or attend the training courses. Tomas reflected on his naivety, blindness and utterly trusting personality. He had loved her dearly. He had no inkling whatsoever of her dissatisfaction with life - with him! Their heart to heart was a shock to his system, the announcement of the end of his marriage a knot in his stomach.

Tomas had experienced three years of capital life before his marriage to Zsofia, sharing a flat with four others. He loved this period, enjoying the fun of the restaurants and bars within walking distance, the ticking of stationary taxis dropping off fares from outside his window, the camaraderie of a group of youngsters living together: telly in the lounge with Greta, Hanna and Istvan, all discovering they had taken the same day off together; Elek's room listening to music, the banter at breakfast, the impromptu visit to the local Goulash Bisztro on a Tuesday evening, a kick around in the park on a Sunday afternoon. Meeting Zsofia was the beginning of a completely different world.

An hour later than planned, the train reduced speed in preparation for its arrival at Pekas, not exactly revealing to those new to the town the more attractive aspects of Pekas, each side of the carriage equally depressing: to the left, rows of backyards and shabby gardens, to the right high banks, bare trees and muddy hills, viewed through windows smeared with the wash of driving rain. The buffet car had closed half an hour earlier, the doors now silent, their lack of activity noticeable as Tomas re-emerged from his thoughts of the past to the reality of the present.

A taxi to the house was an option, but Tomas's body

needed movement. He had sat down for long enough and a forty-five-minute walk would loosen his legs and get his blood flowing again. He walked for about a hundred yards parallel to the station. To the left was the long straight gradual incline that would take him a quarter of the way, past what he remembered would be the more unsavoury element of Pekas. To the right, just about fifty yards away, on the other side of the level crossing, was the Szimpla Ruin Bar. He thought immediately how refreshing a Dreher would be after the journey. It was getting dark and, although only four o'clock, he decided to 'live a bit'. With safety barriers in the raised position, he crossed the tracks and headed for the entrance. Once through the doors, he saw bodies, mostly men grouped in threes and fours, in conversation, some standing with beers in hand, others seated, glasses showing different amounts of remaining contents suggesting slow drinkers or recent arrivals. The unpleasant smell of Hungarian stuffed cabbage brought a grimace to his face, töltött káposzta; it was never his favourite. The interior, certainly quite different to the bar he remembered, had become more café style, with light wooden tables and chairs, equally suited to daytime coffees or evening drinks. Tomas edged forward, excusing himself as he twisted and turned to get past the crowd. Then, coming into view, most unmistakably, sitting on a stool in conversation, was Dev. Tomas stopped in his tracks. No, this is not what he wanted. He immediately turned, hoping he hadn't already been spotted, weaved his way back to where he came from and left. He walked briskly towards the railway crossing which was now flashing its lights and bleeping its audible warning in anticipation of the next train due to pass through. The barriers were just a moment from closing when Tomas sprinted across and marched towards the hill, gradually calming down and reducing his pace. Within five minutes of arriving in Pekas, his doubts and anxieties about his return were already proving to be justified. Feeling the need for some fresh air, he decided to avoid the hill and the miserable memories it would bring back along the way and take the alternative route along the river.

Diverting into Ferenc Street, his eyes widened at the sight ahead of him. The ugly block of flats he had expected to see had been replaced by a modern, waterfront development featuring fashionable shops and trendy restaurants, each with smart frontages, whilst interiors illuminated by ambient lighting provided a warm welcome for patrons. Towards the end of the development, he expected to see the disused, dilapidated, church-like building which once controlled the dock's hydraulic gates, but on arrival discovered it had now been converted to a smart, up-market restaurant serving bisztro-style dishes. His mood lifted. He lingered around the building, peering into the cavernous interior, stylishly modernised but retaining the original stonework. He gazed out on to the river, his thoughts now returning to his train conversation with Dev. Pondering. Questioning. Speculating.

He turned back down Ferenc Street towards the restaurants and shops, hoping there was still time. His brisk walk transformed into a sprint as the barriers appeared in the distance, lowered in readiness for the next train. The temperature registered three degrees on his phone, but Tomas felt exhilarated from the combination of warmth from his exertion, and the cold, fresh air on his face. As he approached the barriers, the train crawled out of the station, Tomas choosing not to wait, but to cross over the pedestrian bridge. When at the top, he looked down and watched the stream of carriages pass beneath him making their way back to Budapest. As he stood there, he recalled standing in the same spot as a child, when the old steam locomotive would pass beneath and release its steam to such an extent that seeing anything on that bridge for several seconds was impossible. In his memory, the steam cleared, and in the present the train sped on towards his previous life. Tomas took eager, quick steps down the bridge, crossed the road, and strode confidently into The Szimplker Ruin Bar. He looked purposefully for Dev, who hadn't moved, still in deep conversation. Tomas tapped him on the shoulder:

"Dev."

"Tomas. Well, bloody hell. You made it."

"Yes, looks like we both had the same idea."

"What are you having? Oh, by the way, this is Jozsef. You won't know him as he only moved here a year ago, but we kept bumping into one another, so we try and meet up when I come down. He's an accountant, like you."

"Hi Jozsef, pleased to meet you," said Tomas reaching out to shake hands. "I'll have a beer thanks Dev, or should I call you Keleman?"

BUBBLES

They'd agreed to meet in an area well known for being one of the true gems of south London: Whittley Street, a perfectly preserved brick terrace from the 1820s used as a location for Victorian and period dramas, and Theed Street which bends sharply round to meet the jagged pitched roofs of Roupel Street; houses that date back to the nineteenth and early twentieth centuries. Bill loved this area, and being in proximity to the new snooker rooms where they were due to play a few frames, he was keen to show his nephew where he spent fifteen years of his career as an English teacher. Turning in to Exton Street, the two men came across The Old School, a perfect example of a Victorian school building, one of many still existing today.

"Well, there it is. I used to teach there thirty-five years ago. Brings back many memories," said Bill looking up at the vast imposing red-brick building.

"You don't get buildings like that anymore," said Adam, standing alongside Bill, both men now gazing upwards. "Must be impressive inside."

"Very much so: high ceilings, huge halls, loads of light."

"The kids you taught must be in their fifties by now."

"Yes, amazing. Time flies. I remember them all so well, and the staff. We were a great team. I can see it now: stairs and corridors packed with kids all trooping up and down for lessons. Certainly kept me fit in those days. The English department was based on the top floor. I must have walked up and down those stairs twenty times a day."

"And now it's mainly walking around the snooker table," quipped Adam, "though I doubt if you'll get much exercise this afternoon, I'm in good form."

"Don't you be so sure of yourself young man. I'm feeling pretty confident myself. See that magpie over there, ready to spread its wings and take to the sky," said Bill, pointing to the black and white, long-tailed warbler perched on the railings, "that's me."

Adam and his uncle had been meeting once a month since Bill's retirement, snooker being a sport they both enjoyed, and Bill appreciative of having a partner with whom he could play on a regular basis. Flexible working enabled Adam to take the odd day off. After ten more minutes of Bill's reminiscing, they continued their stroll.

"How are things then, Adam? How's work?"

"Fine thanks Bill."

"Good."

"Well, actually, as you're asking, I'm thinking of changing career."

Bill's gaze turned towards Adam, eyebrows raised in surprise. "Changing career!"

"Don't look at me like that Bill."

"And what exactly are you thinking of changing to?"

"Well, believe it or not, teaching."

"Teaching!"

"Yes, I fancy working with youngsters. I'm pretty good at my job and the social interaction would suit me."

"But why would you want to give up engineering and go into teaching? You're earning good money. Teachers get pittance."

"Well, why not? Come on Bill, I thought you'd approve of me following in your footsteps. The pay is much better now, and it's a good pension, as you know. Anyway, it's not just about the money. I just think I would enjoy the prospect of standing in front of a class of youngsters passing on my skills and knowledge: maths, computing, analytical thinking. And then there's the whole social aspect of school life. There'll be a bit of a buzz. It just appeals to me. I'm bored in telecommunications. Seven years is enough. I don't think I want to do this for the rest of my life. I want a change. I've been reading up about it. They are crying out for people with my skills. It would be a refreshing change. A new challenge. I thought you'd be pleased for me."

"Well, it will certainly be a challenge. The reality is, you'll spend most of your time trying to control the kids. You'll need your yellow helmet, protective clothing, and hose pipe. If you can't control the kids, it's hopeless, you'll have a miserable time. You're too nice a guy Adam. I'm not sure you're really suited. Especially today with all the issues kids have. Do you really want to be caught up with all that? In my day it was bad enough, but in today's modern world kids are fraught with issues. Childhood has changed. More single parent families, lack of discipline at home, poor parenting, mobile phones, social media. I'm telling you now, you won't enjoy it. You won't be able to actually teach. You've got to be exceptional in today's world. Like Miss Tomkins."

"Miss Tomkins?"

"Yes Miss Tomkins, or Bubbles as the kids used to call her. We learnt so much from her." As Bill was about to tell the story, grey clouds dominated the sky and light rain began to fall. "Looks a bit ominous," said Bill. "Come on, if we quicken the pace, we could dive into the Queen's Head and have a quick pint until things improve."

"Good idea," said Adam.

The Queen's Head, a quintessential real ale south London pub, offered a pleasant and traditional drinking environment, the front space being divided into public and saloon bars and a back area now a restaurant serving Thai food. Displayed around the walls were framed art prints of various sizes depicting works of famous artists.

"This seems an interesting place," said Adam.

"Well, it used to be, but it's changed a lot. Like most pubs now, it's all about the food. All you can smell is chips, burgers, or curry. As soon as those odours hit my nose, I feel a sense of despair at the demise of the proper pub. Come on, I'll buy you a drink."

"Thanks. I'll have a coke please."

"A coke? Have a beer. It's real ale. You can't not have a real ale!"

Before Adam could reply, Bill ordered two pints of Yachtsman. The barman poured the pints and placed them on the bar. Just as Adam reached for his glass, Bill directed his gaze more closely into the beers.

"They look a bit flat. Hardly any head on them."

"Hmm, looks alright to me. That's how they are," said the barman.

Bill takes a sip. "No, definitely flat."

Adam takes a sip. "Seems okay to me."

"No, not for me. A giant panda has more effervescence!" Bill slides the glass back towards the barman. "Could you change it please? In fact, I'll have a pint of West Coast IPA instead."

"Okay, sorry, no problem." The barman takes the glass from Bill, pours its contents away and replaces it with the West Coast. Bill takes a sip and waits a second.

"That's much better. Well, a bit better to be precise, but

it's fine. Thank you."

The two men sat down and made themselves comfortable. Seated beside them were a family of four: mum, dad and two children about eleven or twelve years of age, both sipping lemonades out of straws.

"Do you see what I mean Adam," whispered Bill. "Why bring kids in here? It's not a kids' place."

"Maybe they're just waiting for a table in the restaurant," replied Adam. At that point the mum leaned over towards Adam, holding up her phone.

"Excuse me, sorry to disturb you but would you mind taking a photo?"

"Yes, of course," replied Adam.

"Oh, thanks so much." The lady handed Adam her phone and the family huddled together for the shot.

"Thanks so much."

"No problem," replied Adam returning the phone. "Going somewhere nice?"

"Yes, Madam Tussauds. The kids have always wanted to go."

"Oh, very nice. They'll enjoy that."

"Not sure what the attraction is myself," intervened Bill. "Just a load of waxworks. Not real people."

"Oh, the kids can't wait. They've just reintroduced the Chamber of Horrors," said the lady.

"There's a gastropub across the road from there if you're looking for a bit of darkness, might be cheaper. Only slightly mind you. There'll be queues you know. Have you booked?"

"Yes, so we should be alright."

"I wouldn't bank on that. They'll be winding into Allsopp Place round the corner. Must have cost you a fortune."

"We've got a family ticket."

"Still a rip-off though. Just to see wax works. They're not even that good a likeness. I went when I was a kid. Just a big disappointment. In those days they had the planetarium as well, so you went to both. Much better value for money."

"Well, I'm sure it will be fine. Thanks for your help," said the lady, angling her body away from Bill and returning her attention to her family.

"A pleasure," said Adam. "It's not just about the waxworks you know," said Adam turning back towards Bill. "Kids can learn a lot about history. There are numerous historical characters there. Muhammad Ali, Martin Luther King, Richard Branson. Inspiring people. And it's much better now. They offer experiences, rides, more interaction."

"Still a rip-off in my view. Don't know how families can afford it."

Both men sipped their pints.

"There seems to be quite a few paintings dotted around," said Bill placing his glass back onto the table. "Landlord must be into art. Bit unusual to see in a pub."

"Yes, I've noticed," replied Adam, his attention turning to a framed print of Matisse's *The Snail*.

Bill looked at it, forehead frowned, lips pursed, "Do you know, I'll never really understand all the fuss about that painting, if it is a painting. Or is it just bits of paper? Apparently, it's worth millions! A child could have done it. I don't get it. Funny thing art. Doesn't even look anything like a snail."

"I think there's a bit more to it than that Bill. It's about the balance of composition and harmony of the colours, and the spiral form is meant to be representative of the direction of universal movement. It's the intention behind these things that make them what they are. Yes, a young child can cut out bits of coloured paper and stick them on a contrasting background, but they aren't necessarily trying to express any specific ideas, although never underestimate a child's mind; they've got amazing imaginations."

"Well, that's not going to convince me. Come on look at it. How on earth could that really have any skill in it?"

"Well, you could say that about lots of things," replied Adam pointing to a black and white picture of a urinal above Bill's head. Bill turned around to look up at the framed print.

"Well, that proves my point doesn't it."

"Art isn't necessarily about skill Bill. It's about ideas. That's Marcel Duchamp's *Fountain*. He was into ready-made objects, purchased a urinal, and displayed it on its back rather than in its usual upright position."

"Oh, very clever and…*artistic*," said Bill, raising the first two fingers of each hand in the air signalling quotation marks.

"Yes, but he was challenging the art world when he submitted it for an exhibition, and the beauty of it was that because it was rejected, sanitaryware, certainly not considered to be works of art, became famous for the controversy that followed. It's often the stories behind these things that give art its value."

"Well, it's all a mystery to me. Anyway, talking about toilets has made me want to go to the loo. Be back in a sec." Bill rose from his seat and headed off briskly towards the gents situated at the end of the restaurant area. In the meantime, the Madam Tussauds family had finished their drinks and stood up to leave, mum thanking Adam for the photo, and set off for their adventure with the waxed celebs. A few minutes later Bill reappeared.

"Bit of a state in there. Grubby, no soap, and the hand-dryer doesn't work. Lets the pub down. You can always tell a lot about a place from the toilets. It can be as grand or as beautifully decorated as you like but if the loos are rubbish it mars your whole opinion. You wonder what the kitchen's like."

"Actually, that reminds me," said Adam. "Good news. Work on my extension is starting next week. It will give me a much larger kitchen than the poky one I've got now. A lot more space. And it will add value to the property."

"Yes, but be prepared for weeks of upheaval first," replied Bill. "How long have they said it will take?"

"Two months."

"Right, expect four. Oh, and make sure they've checked the foundations, or the walls will be cracking before you know it."

"Oh, I'm sure it will be fine Bill. I've had all the plans properly done. It will be worth it in the end."

"And don't assume it will add value. Property prices have peaked. In fact, you could even end up in negative equity."

"I'm sure it will be fine Bill. They'll be back up. Anyway, what about this story you were going to tell me? Miss Tomkins. Bubbles."

"Ah yes, Bubbles. She was the Science teacher. She joined the school in her third year of teaching. We'd already heard gossip that things hadn't been going well for her; she was on the verge of giving up teaching altogether.

The bottom line was, she couldn't control the kids. Her first term with us was a nightmare. All her energies went towards controlling behaviour instead of creating inspiring lessons. Actually, not dissimilar to that picture there," said Bill pointing to *A School for Boys and Girls* by Jan Steen depicting an unruly bunch of children causing chaos in the classroom: shouting, laughing, fighting, singing, sprawling across chairs, standing on desks, the floor littered with torn and screwed up paper. Adam looked up at the painting. "We all knew she couldn't cope, and once the kids knew she couldn't cope she'd had it. Nothing she did worked. Though she never went so far as to send the kids to the head. That would be evidence of her weakness. She would have been sending kids every day! She knew her subject though - excellent qualifications - but just couldn't control the children. She simply seemed to be one of those teachers who didn't have that 'something' that made the children connect with her. Too weak, a soft touch, someone to take advantage of, one of those teachers who children will eat for breakfast. She'd spend every day telling them off, keeping them in at playtime, detention, sending them out of the classroom, giving them lines, negativity creating further negativity. She obviously wasn't a natural. She was just a mild-mannered person, nice, pleasant, but these were not the qualities that would create a learning environment. Then one day everything changed."

As Bill was about to continue, Adam noticed two other paintings displayed across the room: Gustave Courbet's *Le Désespéré*, depicting the artist as a young man in despair, eyes wide open, as if eagerly anticipating Bill's continuation of the story, and Acrimboldo's *German Emperor Rudolf 11*, composed of plant and vegetable matter: green beans for eyebrows, red fruits for lips, apples for cheeks, a pear for the nose.

"Miss Tomkins is at her desk trying to discuss a piece of work with one of her pupils when she notices soap bubbles at the back of the classroom floating towards the ceiling. After a few seconds the kids start giggling, gradually rising to a peak of uproarious laughter. 'Alright, who's got the bubbles?' she says, looking in the direction of Amanda Morris.

'Miss, don't look at me. It's not me,' says Amanda. She turns her attention towards Josie Sinclair, eyes narrowing, cheeks reddening.

'Miss, it's not me, no way,' she says.

Then, she threatens to keep everyone in for break if no-one owns up. The kids moan and complain. Then Freddie Fenshaw stands up, the class goes silent, and he's loving the attention.

'It's me Miss.'

'Right, give them to me right now Freddie,' says Miss Tomkins.

Freddie saunters to the front of the class, blows another burst of soap in final defiance, and hands the small container, with bubble wand, over to Miss Tomkins. She puts them in her drawer.

'Right Freddie, it's detention for you. You will be expected in room seventeen after school on Thursday.'

'Yes, Miss. I'll be there,' calls out Freddie already returning to his seat, kids laughing, murmuring, hands banging on tables.

'Right, that's enough. Now get on with your work, all of you, or you'll all be joining Freddie on Thursday.' The noise abates and the children return to their task."

"All sounds crazy," interjected Adam. "Poor Miss Tomkins. I do remember some weak teachers myself when I was at school. It was awful. You could never get your work done or if it was something nice, something fun, like a games lesson, we'd all have to sit it in the hall and miss out just because of a few disruptive pupils spoiling everything."

"Exactly. The point being, Miss Tomkins wasn't in control. The kids were."

"Yes, of course, you're right."

"Anyway, the next morning, the class stroll in as usual, heading for their seats, chatting away. Freddie Fenshaw is first to spot a small cluster of transparent *floating, featherlight spheres* (Bill exaggerates the alliteration) drifting towards the huge wooden sash window."

'Miss, there's bubbles over there!' says Freddie, arm fully extended, pointing.

'What? Oh, yes, so there are. Now never mind that and sit down.'

'Hey, I bet those are mine,' says Freddie. 'Miss, you've been blowing my bubbles, haven't you? Come on Miss, admit it.' The classroom is in uproar.

'Alright. Stop.' There is no response. She raises her hands in the air and shouts, 'Stop!' The class is silent. 'Alright, I admit it,' she says. 'When I came in this morning, I found them in my drawer and just couldn't resist having a go. I used to love them as a child, and it just brought back a few memories.'

'Detention Miss,' shouts out Jimmy Jenkins. The class roar with laughter.

'Alright. Alright that's enough. Look, if you all settle

down and sit quietly, I'll get the bubbles out and blow them.'

The kids settle down. She takes the bubble container out of the drawer, unscrews the wand, and starts to blow. Of course, they all go crazy again and try and burst the bubbles. After they had all dispersed, they eventually settle down to the lesson. And they actually worked! They'd released all their mischievous energy so early, they now focused on their task. After about fifteen minutes things began to stir again, Freddie Fenshaw keen for a repeat of Bubbles' performance.

'Come on Miss, blow the bubbles again.'

'Freddie, that's enough. Get on with your work. We've had enough disruption already.' There's silence. Miss Tomkins stares at the class but the murmuring begins to rise.

'I'll tell you what I'll do. At the very end of the lesson, I'll blow the bubbles again, as long as you carry on working as you have done and leave the classroom in silence.'

The class carry on working, and at the end of the lesson, she gets out the bubbles, blows them, and the kids all leave in silence, the bubbles floating around them like *celestial orbs of calming chamomile.*

As they walk in the next morning, the room is full of bubbles, Miss Tompkins is standing there holding a sign: STAY SILENT, ENJOY THE BUBBLES AND SIT IN YOUR SEATS. The novelty is now out of their system, and they are enjoying the more serene nature of the bubbles. The kids did exactly as the sign said. After the register, she began to explain how bubbles are formed."

"Ah, I know this Sir," interrupted Adam raising his

hand as if in the classroom. "Soap molecules have two different ends: one attracts water, and the other repels water. When soap mixes with water, the opposite ends of the soap molecules sandwich a thin layer of water between themselves."

"Precisely. Well done, Adam. Anyway, as I was saying, the children were…"

"This creates a thin film that surrounds a tiny bit of air. A bubble! So, when you look at a bubble, what you're seeing is a tiny bit of air trapped inside a thin film composed of two layers of soap molecules encasing a thin layer of water."

"I couldn't have put it better myself. Thank you, Adam. Now, if you'll let me continue?"

"Yes, sorry Uncle; I got carried away."

"The children were transfixed. And when it came to doing the follow up work in their books, they all worked purposefully. And from then on everything changed. The bubbles became part of the daily routine. Because they were focused on their tasks, Miss Tomkins now had the chance to give them more individual attention. This in turn enabled them to experience her real teaching qualities and expertise in her subject knowledge. She was able to focus more on what they were achieving in the lesson., noticing every small improvement. She simply had more time to spend with individual children, positively finding the best in them. They loved the attention, and as they became used to her recognising all the good things in their work, they became more used to her methods. She would often stop the class as she walked around helping them and ask individuals to read out their work, or to explain an experiment they had carried out and talk about what they were trying to achieve. She ensured that every one of them regularly had the opportunity to talk about their work during the week. And when one of them did step out of line, it was never about consequences; she would encourage them to reflect on their actions and, through that, they matured. At first, she maintained the use of the bubbles, but gradually she withdrew them, without the kids even noticing. They had become used to working in a purposeful atmosphere, responding to Bubbles' non-judgemental approach to their behaviour, accomplishments, and choices. They were building self-confidence and developing an independent sense of worth."

"Quite an amazing transformation," said Adam. "I see what you mean now, about actually teaching."

"All the children would look forward to having Bubbles. Whenever she had a new class, she would start off with the bubbles and the kids would respond even though they knew why she was doing it. They all loved having Bubbles and the working environment she created: her positive nature, her fun, her encouragement. And her success and transformation were certainly recognised by the school as there was a distinct change in other teachers' approaches in the following years. Yes, I was lucky to witness this and be part of that transformation: the concept of motivating kids through nurturing and finding the positive rather than through punishment, consequences, and negativity. I think I must have got my timing just right in that school."

"That's quite a story, Bill. Looks like going into teaching's worth considering quite seriously then."

"Goodness me no. It's a different world today. As I

said earlier, childhood has changed. Kids have so many emotional problems these days. They are more challenging, more defiant, more aware of their rights. No, teachers like Bubbles are rare; you must have an exceptional personality, something a bit different. No offence Adam but I don't think you have that 'something extra'. Oh, yes, then there's Government inspections, constant monitoring by the head, targets. No, teachers haven't got a chance these days. Morale is low. They have to take on so many emotional and pastoral responsibilities. You may as well go and work in social services. Do you know how many are leaving the profession every year? Nearly half of teachers plan to quit after five years in the profession! And seventy per cent of those are because of the stress over children's behaviour! Vital time is lost. I'm telling you now, don't do it."

"Surely this is more reason to do it," said Adam. "They need people like Bubbles. They need someone to believe in them, to find the best in them, particularly the type of kids you've been talking about."

"Adam, believe me, in two years you'll regret it. You'll be stressed out and wondering why on earth you made the change."

"But I'll never know unless I give it a go. I'm not sure I want to be in telecommunications all my life. Didn't you wish you had done something different instead of being in the same job for forty years?"

"Adam, there's a lot to be said for staying in the same job. You know where you stand. Security, pension, working your way up the ladder. Think about it Adam. What if it all goes wrong? What if you're not suited? You're not a Bubbles. And then what? You'll have to think about what to do after that. Return to telecommunications? Or maybe you'll try something different with maybe no option but to take a reduction in salary."

"Hmm, maybe you're right," replied Adam. "I'll have a serious think about it tonight. Weigh up the pros and cons."

"I would if I was you. It will affect your whole future. Anyway, we must move on. We've got five frames to fit in. Drink up."

Adam finished his last drop of beer and both men ventured back out to the gloomy streets, the clouds black, and the rain pouring hard.

"Bloody hell, can't see this abating Adam, probably going to be like this for a few days. Most likely will have to cancel my weekend in the caravan. Come on, let's go; we may as well stroll, going to get a soaking anyway." Adam and Bill set off for their afternoon session.

Having gone their separate ways following their snooker extravaganza, Adam sat silently in the tube carriage, deep in thought. Once home, he made himself dinner, continuing to ponder over his future and his conversation with his uncle. Following a desert of fruit salad, he turned on the tap, squirting in washing-up liquid simultaneously, creating a froth of soapsuds to wash the dishes. As he placed the squeezy plastic bottle back on the draining board, a large bubble formed at its tip, and as quickly as it appeared, broke away and floated upward, the ceiling spotlight revealing its hidden rainbow. Adam stared in fixed-gaze fashion as it gradually travelled higher, struck the hard surface, burst, and disappeared.

THE HARPIST

The small village of Ashwood, a popular wedding location for all seasons, lies beside the River Thyme, which almost surrounds the village in a triangular fashion, featuring a distinctive curve along the north side. At the centre lies the church where the ceremony had taken place just thirty minutes earlier. The approach to Ashwood is famous for its five mile long ridge of common land, where the experience of the lost joys of motoring are reborn with an undulating stretch of country road, free from motorway mayhem, providing rare opportunities for rollercoaster thrills and spills with stunning views of countryside and of distant coastline, though drivers would always need to be prepared to put on the brakes in anticipation of roaming sheep and wild ponies drifting a little too close to the road. At the end of the stretch, more frequent bends become the key feature until the arrival at Ashwood, and the reason for most people's journey along this road: The King Harry, a wedding venue, hotel, and traditional country inn with log fires, cosy restaurant, and a relaxed and friendly old pub atmosphere. Such is its popularity that it is regularly fully booked throughout the year, and the reason for its popularity is the owner Abigail Harper, known for her love of love and passion for people.

Abigail Harper has always kept herself in good shape. Now in her mid-thirties, she has retained her size eight throughout the years. She has pride in her appearance, dressing smartly every day to meet her prospective clients: white blouse, black jacket, ankle length tailored trousers and sling back high heels, or should more colour be the order of the day, a plum, short-sleeved fitted knee length dress. With blessed good looks and a healthy skin, a minimum of make-up was all that she felt she needed, and her new sleek black bob hairstyle suited her perfectly. She had a knack of connecting with people, making them feel at ease, understanding their needs, drawing on inspiration from couples' own stories of how they met, how they became engaged, or from their family histories. The previous weekend, she incorporated Florida shaped cookies into the décor and food for a couple who met in Miami Beach, the comfort and enjoyment of guests always paramount.

The King Harry provided a perfect balance of country pub essentials: ample seating, a bar catering for a wide variety of ales, and an extensive menu to suit every palate. An outside area, perfect for the late spring heatwave, dedicated itself to Alice and Rob's happy occasion which had reached that time when there is an extensive gap between the ceremony and reception dinner: the cocktail hour, providing opportunity for guests to relax, mingle, sip drinks and sample the wide variety of food on offer, and to enjoy the display of typical wedding outfits: women in their floral wraps and lace detail bodycons, men in their three-piece suits of blues, blacks and greys. Abigail's magic touch was everywhere, something for everyone to feel amazed and inspired by her choices. Globally influenced by the bride and groom's love of travel, Abigail had ensured an eclectic mix of dishes was on offer to please a wide range of tastes. The two waiters, rocks of the earth, especially selected by Abigail for this occasion, dedicated themselves to ensuring everyone was filled with sparkling goodness, while the enticing food stations provided happiness in all its succulent glory: cheese and charcuterie boards, pasta, pizza, oysters, shrimps, sushi and clams. The garden was laid out with both high-top tables and low seating options to cater for everyone's personal preference to stand or sit. On the specially constructed stage, a harpist was setting up in preparation for a performance of cascading glissandos.

Standing with a mixed plate of hors d'oeuvres was Isabella Jackson, a fine musician and close friend of the bride, married to George, and mother of Andrew and Charlotte, aged nine and thirteen respectively. Music is Isabella's life, learning to play the violin from the age of eight, becoming sufficiently accomplished to join the school orchestra at fifteen and now twenty years later a valued member of the Gabriel Philharmonia. She had descended from a long line of musicians within the family: her father a pianist, her mother a flautist, her grandparents singers, and her great-grandparents music hall entertainers. She wished more than anything for her children to follow the family tradition. Andrew had developed an enthusiasm for the keyboard having responded positively to his mother's encouragement. Charlotte, however, appeared to have no passion for learning an instrument whatsoever, Isabella having tried everything to stimulate interest but without success.

Over at the beer cooler stood Raymond Wainwright, not the sort of man who enjoys these occasions: adhering to protocols, rules of etiquette and making conversation with people he doesn't know, or perhaps whom he may subconsciously believe are above his station. He'd far rather be in his local with his drinking associates having a few lagers and watching football or singing along with the local band. He only tolerated these events for the sake of his wife Jean, who loved any excuse for free drinks and food. Indeed, he loved the free drinks too, but never took a liking to the fancy cuisine on offer: prosciutto and freshly shaved parmesan, watermelon cubes with burrata and balsamic vinegar, seared tuna with wasabi seaweed salad; burger and chips would always be preferable. However, recent health issues have caused him some concern, notably high blood pressure and sleep problems, not surprising considering the stress he has been recently under due to lack of work opportunities and subsequent financial challenges. Rapid weight gain hasn't helped. He has been seeing his doctor and is on a course of medication. Jean, a great believer in aromatherapy, has tried to encourage him to spend more time dedicated to body, mind and spirit, but to no avail.

Then there's Jonathan Mitchell, the broad-shouldered man spruced up in the red, white, and black pin-striped shirt. A keen sportsman, extremely fit, tall and muscular, rugged good looks, and a good head of hair, usually styled in a high-flying quiff. He had wandered off to the perimeter of the lawn, a solitary figure looking pensively into the distance,

The performance was about to begin when Abigail Harper appeared from the doorway and approached him.

"Hello. Are you alright, if you don't mind me asking?"

"Oh, hello. Yes thanks, I'm just feeling a little queasy. I'm sure I'll be alright in a minute."

"Are you with anyone?"

"No, it's just me."

"Okay, well, look, why don't you come inside to cool

down?"

"Um, okay, yes, thanks, I will. Probably a good idea."

"Come on, follow me."

On the stage, the harpist was poised to begin. It was a magnificent instrument, its renowned triangular shape enhanced by the curved mahogany upper neck and majestic gold leaf fore-pillar, exquisitely adorned with floral decals. Raising her arms simultaneously and focusing her eyes on the strings, she reached forward, placed her hands in the starting position and began her opening piece: a harp solo from Donizetti's *Lucia di Lammermoor*, instantly creating beautiful tones and harmonious togetherness, her delicate fingers gliding across the breadth of the harp like gentle waves lapping the shore. Her long brown hair fell elegantly onto one shoulder, settling on her light beige chiffon blouse, its wide tailored sleeves waving in time with the music.

Abigail and Jonathan made their way into a cool quiet room, away from the merriment and music, with two black leather wingback chairs facing each other. Jonathan sat upright on the edge of the seat, hands clasped on his lap. Abigail sat opposite, mirroring his position.

"Is there anything I can get you? By the way, I'm Abigail, the hotel owner."

"Hello Abigail, pleased to meet you. I'm Jonathan. No thanks. I'm sorry about all this. Just give me a few minutes."

"Okay, no problem. There's no rush."

Raising both hands to his face, Jonathan rubbed his cheeks, cleared a tear from each eye, breathed in deeply, and blew heavily through his lips.

"Would you like to talk? Can I help in any way? I'm a

good listener."

"No thanks, honestly, I'll be fine." Jonathan widened his eyes and stretched his mouth open, releasing the tension from his facial muscles, gradually pulling himself together.

"Okay, that's alright. Take your time."

As Jonathan gained control over his emotions, more confidence creeping in, he felt ready to share his troubles.

"Actually, yes, it would be nice to talk, if you really don't mind."

"Okay, good, that's fine. Let me fetch you a glass of water."

The lower murmur of the guests had ceased as they became consumed within the harpist's aura of beautiful confidence.

Abigail returned with the water to find Jonathan now leaning back in his chair appearing more relaxed. She sat down and made herself comfortable in a similar position, her self-assurance, attention, and beauty making him feel at ease and ready to open his heart.

"The fact is, Alice and I used to be together."

"Oh…I see…" said Abigail, instantly understanding the cause for Jonathan's distress.

"We were engaged. This was meant to be my day. I thought I'd be fine, but I'm not. Everyone said we were the 'perfect couple', then she started a new job and met Rob! That was a year ago."

Abigail raised her eyebrows, completely taken by surprise. It was obvious that Alice and Rob hadn't revealed the whole story in their preparations for the reception. She remained silent, allowing Jonathan time to continue.

"Just colleagues at first. Drinks after work, that sort of

thing. Then the bombshell. She wanted to be with him."

"I'm sorry to hear all this Jonathan. This can't be an easy time for you. No wonder you're upset."

"She said she was confused, still loved me. Looking back, she was obviously trying to let me down gently. I was patient and tried to understand what was going on. I loved her even though she wanted someone else. I didn't want to let go, but in the end I had no choice."

"But you're here today?"

"Yes. We stayed friends. After the initial shock, I accepted the situation, or at least let Alice believe I had. The truth is, I was always hoping she would ultimately change her mind, that she would break up with him. Selfish of me really. But that's how I felt."

"This must be very difficult for you, being here right now. It was brave of you to come," said Abigail, her soft tones allowing Jonathan to feel a sense of calm and assurance in her presence. A few moments of silence ensued, Abigail deliberately not interrupting, enabling Jonathan to process his thoughts and feelings.

"I shouldn't have come really. It was stupid of me. I thought I'd be fine. I've had plenty of time to get over it, but the fact is I haven't. It's probably best I leave."

"Do you know anyone here?" asked Abigail.

"I know a few people."

"Well then, why not stay. It may be the best thing to do. See it through. It may help the healing process, seeing how happy she is, and Rob. That's a good thing, isn't it?"

"Yes, I suppose so. I don't know, I'll see how it goes. Maybe stay for the speeches. That will certainly bring things to a conclusion. If I can get through those it'll be an achievement."

"Maybe then you can draw a line under it. Move on."

"Yes, I suppose so. You're right. I've got to put all this behind me. The wedding has finalised things in a way. She's married now, that's it."

"I'm assuming you haven't met anyone since the break-up?"

"No, I've kept myself to myself. I've had no desire to be with anyone else. I've lived in the hope that ultimately, we'd be back together."

"What will you do next? I mean, after today?"

"Just get on with it I suppose. Distract myself. Get back to work. Keep busy."

"That's a good start. What do you do if you don't mind me asking?"

"Not at all. Nothing particularly exciting. I'm an accountant."

"Oh, I'm sure there are fascinating aspects to the job. A good accountant is worth the world. I can vouch for that. What do you do for fun?"

"Sport mainly, and photography, though I don't get much chance to pursue that side of things."

"Sounds great. Is it possible for you to take a break? It would do you good to get away from everything."

"I suppose I could."

"Do something active, as you're into sport. Keep your mind off things. How about skiing? I've just come back from Val d'Isere. It was amazing. That would be perfect. Have you ever been?"

"I've been a couple of times. It is good fun. Bit late in the season though."

"Not at all; there are plenty of great places to go in April. It'll do you wonders. Give you some breathing space. Mountains, fresh air, exhilaration. Take some photos. They'll be great. You'll come back a new man."

"Maybe I will. You're right. I need to get away from it all. Have some fun."

Jonathan felt fully at ease in Abigail's company as she listened intently: nodding, agreeing, responding in soft gentle timbre, maintaining eye contact. She sensed the stress and tension stored in his body gradually ease as he unloaded his troubles. He in turn sensed Abigail's tenderness and warmth through her tone of voice and relaxed facial expression, perfectly framed by her straight black bob giving her an air of sophistication and elegance.

The harpist continued her piece, gracefully raising and lowering her head and shoulders, spreading her delicate palms across the strings, producing wonderful harmonies to entrance the audience, now fully focused on the grandeur before their eyes.

"You *will* meet someone again, Jonathan. Yes, you've experienced the pain of lost love. Embrace that pain. It will help you move on. And you will love again. It will rise and declare its glory. Right now, Jonathan, there's a beautiful woman out there just waiting to be presented with a bouquet of red roses – by you."

"Maybe," said Jonathan, nodding, a hint of a smile emerging. He reached for his water and took a sip. Abigail remained silent. "Anyway, look, enough about me. I'll be fine. You've been brilliant. I'm sure I'll sort myself out. What about you? Married? Kids? If you don't mind me asking."

"No, not at all," replied Abigail, herself feeling a heightened sense of ease and lightness. I'm single, and fine with it. My priority has been to get this hotel firmly established. I'm totally committed to the point where I've put romance on the back burner," said Abigail.

"Okay, fair enough," said Jonathan. "Relationships can take up a lot of time and attention."

A few moments of stillness followed, Jonathan and Abigail feeling a quiet sense of contentment in each other's company.

The harpist had captivated the guests to the point where conversations had ceased, the faculties of seeing and hearing now dominant within every invitee's human bounty of gifts, her playing visually beautiful – a majestic, luminous scene emitting an incandescent love for music.

Isabella and George Jackson adored it, enthralled by the splendour on show, as indeed was Charlotte Jackson, mesmerised by the harpist's graceful fingers effortlessly producing pure notes entwined with masterful musicianship, her body unconsciously swaying from side to side. She glanced up towards her parents and smiled, her bright eyes and wide lips crinkling at the corners communicating pleasure and delight. Isabella took hold of Charlotte's hand and squeezed, understanding Charlotte's expressive message.

Raymond Wainwright had at first pulled out his mobile phone to look at the sport section but found himself placing it back into his pocket, hypnotised by the vision before him. Initially it was the harpist's beauty and elegance that caught his eye, certainly a more pleasurable image than the football scores. Gradually, quavers and crotchets assumed centre stage and danced in the forefront of his mind, while thoughts of Jean's tales of meditation and mindfulness transported him into a dream-like state: *He is at the banks of a fast-flowing stream, final demands and all unpleasantness floating to a distant waterfall, his financial troubles disappearing over the cascading crest. A sense of total serenity permeates his body as he bathes in the warm waters of an Icelandic spa, blood flowing freely through his veins.* Jean glanced towards him, confused at first by what she was witnessing, but subsequently moved when recognising an expression of bliss. She kissed him on the cheek and gently placed her arm around his shoulder not wishing to disturb his pleasure.

"Actually, that's not true," declared Abigail.

"Pardon?"

"What I said about being single. I'm not fine with it. I'd love to be married."

"Oh," said Jonathan, slightly startled by Abigail's sudden revelation. "So, what's holding you back?"

"Fear."

"Fear?"

"Yes, fear that that a husband and children will have a negative impact on the quality of what I want to deliver. I'll be caught up with family commitments. As you've just said, relationships need a lot of attention. I won't have time to provide the personal touches that are so important to me. I am passionate about my hotel, about my business, about making special days for all the couples I meet. It's a wonderful feeling. I feel so lucky to have a job that gives me so much joy. I don't want anything to come in the way of it. And worse than anything, I fear that, should marriage not work out, I'll lose everything."

"You haven't found the right one," said Jonathan assuredly. "You must have had lots of admirers?"

"Yes, I have, but I've always put up the barriers. It goes

so far and then I bring it to an end."

"That's what I mean. *You* bring it to an end. They haven't taken you to that next level. That certainty. That feeling that you know he's the one. With Alice, I had no doubts whatsoever. I wanted to marry her, spend the rest of my life with her. And when you get to that point, all your thoughts about losing your business will disappear. You'll take the risk. Though if you're in love it isn't a risk. It will be where you want to go. You'll make it work. With a husband and with children."

Abigail remained silent, eyes fixed on Jonathan's, assimilating his words, astonished that this man, just a few moments earlier at the depths of despair, is now giving her words of wisdom, and making perfect sense!

"You make it sound so easy."

"It is easy. Relax, allow yourself to love. Let go of the shackles. Wash away the fears. As you said yourself, love will rise and declare its glory."

"Ah, you've got me there. Yes, I must take my own advice. Definitely lots to mull over. Now, we must get back to you," insisted Abigail. "How are you feeling?"

"Much better thanks. I should get back out there. I've taken up enough of your time and I'm sure you need to get on and ensure your guests are well looked after."

"Yes, you're right. It's been a pleasure Jonathan," said Abigail rising from her chair. "Enjoy the rest of the day."

As the harpist was completing her final piece, bringing all resonance to an end, Jonathan reappeared outside, headed straight towards the charcuterie board, picked up a black olive with his thumb and forefinger and placed it on his tongue. He chewed around the stone, removed it from his mouth and discarded it into the pit bowl provided.

After another twenty minutes the cocktail hour had come to an end and the guests gathered for the rest of the day's proceedings: the photographs, the dinner, the speeches. Not everyone was able to stay for the evening do. At seven o'clock Jonathan Mitchel decided to make his journey home.

"Hi Jonathan, just caught you. All okay? How did the speeches go?"

"Oh, hi Abigail. Yes, Fine thanks. All good. Going to get off now. Thanks once again for all your help today. You've been amazing."

"That's a pleasure Jonathan. Anytime. Actually, I'm having a bit of a do myself in a few weeks. Would you like to come along? You could take some photos for my portfolio."

"Me? Are you sure?"

"Absolutely sure. I'd love you to come. And if you're interested, you can help me prepare for my next wedding," she said, gazing directly into his eyes.

After some skilful manoeuvring to exit the car park, he set off back along the winding roads and towards the ridge. On reaching the summit, he was brought to a standstill by several sheep crossing the road and decided to pull to the verge, take in some fresh air, and admire the view. No matter how many times he had travelled this way, he was always inspired by the panorama of greens and yellows extending for miles, until the inevitable meeting with the calm, blue-grey sea, itself merging with the sunset sky. He was alerted to a particularly persistent bleat emanating from an area near a small hedge. Peering in the direction of the noise, he spotted a lone sheep walking in circles. It looked rather weighty and, considering the time of year, Jonathan concluded that it must be pregnant. It began to paw the ground with its front feet, bleating loudly; something was imminent. It sat down for a few moments and stood up again. Jonathan gradually edged closer, more detail coming into view. Liquid oozed from its rear end while the pacing, sitting down, standing up and persistent bleating became more urgent. At this point he could hear the distant sound of an engine gradually getting louder. He turned around and could see an all-terrain three-wheeler approaching across the field. Within minutes it arrived, and the man, with tanned complexion, grey hair at the sides and bald on top, wearing well-worn jeans and sweat-stained dark green T-shirt, stepped down.

"No sign of any lambs yet then?" he asked in a broad Cornish accent, not really looking at Jonathan but heading straight towards the struggling ewe.

"Um, no. Any minute now though, I suspect," said Jonathan.

"Let's have a look."

The man, whom Jonathan presumed to be the local farmer, approached the ewe, inspected its progress and then, quite suddenly, with two hands, confidently heaved it over onto its side.

"I think it's going to need a little help," said the farmer.

At this point his right hand disappeared into the ewe's rear end, now revealing a bloated, slimy blood-stained sack. "Just trying to find its legs…ah, got them." The farmer then proceeded to pull firmly, and, with some strength required to complete the task, the lamb appeared, sliding out like a child emerging from a slippery water flume. He then cleared its nose, rubbed its body, and dragged it nonchalantly round to the mother's mouth whose immediate instinct was to lick its body.

"Okay, let's check if there's another. There are usually at least two."

Jonathan continued to stare in amazement. In the farmer's hand went again, searching for the next pair of legs, fiddling around like a hand rummaging inside a feely bag trying to guess its contents.

"Here we go." Another pull, rub, drag and lick and the second lamb is born.

"Just going to check if there's any more."

"Triplets?" Jonathan asked, eyes wide in wonder.

"Ah, yes, just got to find its second leg…got it…here we go." Pull, rub, drag, lick - the third lamb expertly delivered safely.

"One more check." He rummaged around. "No, I think that's it."

"Are you sure?" Jonathan asked.

"Yep, I'm sure. All done."

Jonathan lingered a little longer to see the lambs settle. The bonding process was now in full flow, the lambs already attempting to stand on their wobbly legs.

"Thanks for letting me watch this. It's been amazing," said Jonathan.

"No problem," said the farmer. "Mind you, might not be here for much longer."

"Oh," said Jonathan.

"Might have to sell up. Financial pressures, difficult winters, droughts, costs. I've already had to sell some of my breeding ewes. And to top it all my wife has recently passed away. She looked after all the business side of things. I haven't a clue as to where exactly we are financially, other than I know it's not good."

"I'm sorry to hear all this." said Jonathan furrowing his brows. "Look, let me help you. I'm an accountant. Maybe I can do a review for you. Find a way forward. No charge."

"What? Are you serious?"

"Yes, honestly, no problem. I'll give you my card." Jonathan reached for his wallet from inside his jacket pocket and handed it over. "Jonathan Mitchel. Call me."

"I will. Thank you, said the farmer. "By the way it's Frank."

Jonathan thanked Frank once again for allowing him to stay to witness such a wondrous event and returned to the car to continue his journey home.

LOVE ME AS I LOVE YOU

It was six o'clock. Time for Marcus James to venture out to his local pub and enjoy the warmth of a beautiful summer's evening, its beer garden being the perfect venue to satisfy his desire to drink and relax within the company of strangers. He relished his single life, deciding for himself when he wanted to go out, who he wanted to meet, where he wanted to go and how long he wanted to stay. No accountability. Even his job as Vice President of Marketing at Raybourne Consultants offered him a relative amount of freedom to choose when to work and when to take time out, enabling him to live a good life: an attractive city apartment overlooking the Thames, a top of the range Porsche 718 Spider Convertible and abundant spare cash to spend as he liked allowing him to purchase the finest clothes, dine in the best restaurants, and take numerous European trips each year. These activities would include friends and girlfriends, but most of the time his choice would be to dine solo, fly solo and drive solo, and mostly they would be rewards for his achievements within his professional or personal goals, his most recent being a table for one in Maison François for completing a tandem skydive at thirteen thousand feet.

"Two pints of 1664 please."

"Certainly Sir."

Marcus placed his phone on the table and leant back in his chair. The subsequent moments were all about the anticipation of that first spectacular sensation of the cold, smooth, mellow liquid hitting his lips, and the tantalising crisp flavour passing along his tongue cascading down his throat like a subterranean waterfall. The two beers arrived. He raised the first glass to his mouth and in a few seconds half the pint disappeared in the first gulp and the other half in the second, the golden yellow liquid deliciously quenching his eager thirst.

"Oh my God, beautiful." He reached for the second pint. This time a sip would be sufficient. He could then settle down, relax, and enjoy the pleasures of a cool, slow beer.

A few tables away, he couldn't help but notice two women in conversation, clearly twins, each holding a glass of Pimm's, their jet-black hair and white linen sleeveless summer dresses creating a dazzling vision of summer delight. He wasn't going to let this opportunity go. Pint in hand, he ambled over.

As he approached, their facial features burst into life: high cheek bones, bold cherry lips, glistening white teeth, eyes to die for.

"Excuse me," glancing from one to the other in turn, "I'm sorry to interrupt you but would you mind if I joined you? I've been sitting on my own and I wouldn't mind some company."

"Oh, um, okay, sure, take a seat," agreed the twins, instantly impressed by Marcus's confident manner, good looks, smart casual dress, and fine trim figure.

"Thanks, I'm Marcus," he said reaching out his hand.

"Hi Marcus. I'm Hannah."

"And I'm Emma. Nice to meet you."

Following the initial pleasantries, the conversation moved on to a variety of topics, invariably leading to a discussion about the nature of being identical twins.

"Apart from your looks, are you the same in other ways

or are you completely different people?" asked Marcus. Hannah was first to respond.

"Growing up, mum and dad always wanted to separate us believing that this was the best way for us to develop our own personalities, but regardless of their efforts we were always naturally drawn to one another."

"We found that we excelled at the same things and disliked the same things," added Emma.

"We both did gymnastics, learnt the violin, loved the same books…"

"…the list was endless."

"We used to mess around at school and switch classes," said Hannah, mischievously glancing towards Emma.

"That was great fun. The students would always know but the teachers didn't."

"And boyfriends at university – that was such a laugh too," added Hannah.

"Oh God yes, I hadn't thought of that," said Marcus. "Could they really not tell? Surely, there must be some differences – voice, the way you speak, slightly different tones?"

"Honestly, they couldn't," said Emma, giggling. "What was particularly good fun was when we would double date for the first time. We would swap half-way through after going to the loo together and they never knew the difference."

"And what about knowing what each other's thinking? Does that happen?" asked Marcus.

"Mostly when we speak to each other, we tend to…"

"…finish off each other's sentences."

A good rapport was established during the conversation, and on the twins' departure they swapped numbers agreeing to keep in touch. Marcus made his way home via the local supermarket on Radnor Road unable to resist purchasing his favourite chocolate bar which he loved to eat after a few beers. He would always purchase two – one to eat on the way home and one to savour during his late-night movie.

God, they're both so lovely, he thought. And such good company – great conversationalists, so positive in their outlook and great sense of humour. I've got to ask one of them to dinner, but which one? I'll toss a coin. Heads for Emma, tails for Hannah. He placed the coin on his forefinger, flicked it into the air with his thumb, caught it with the same hand and flipped it on to the back of the other. Hannah.

The chosen restaurant was Benny's Brasserie. Marcus waited excitedly at the bar for Hannah's arrival. On entering, he wasn't disappointed. Wearing an off the shoulder black dress matched with black stilettos and sleek pale pink clutch, she greeted him with a beaming smile and a kiss on the cheek. He ordered a large Pino Grigio and immersed himself in the joy of being in the company of such a beautiful woman. Twenty minutes later they took their seats at the dinner table and continued their conversation.

"So, what did Emma feel about me asking you out and not her? Was she offended in any way?"

"No, not at all. We're both used to it. It often goes fifty-fifty. Obviously if we meet anyone when we are alone there is never an issue because the guy hasn't met the twin. But when we are together, and we meet someone, he never really knows which one to ask out. They discover we are the same in every way and can't find that subtle difference

81

that may cause them to choose one of us over the other. But we're fine with it. It's fun."

Marcus nodded in acknowledgement.

"So, tell me then, why did you choose me?" continued Hannah, leaning forward, gazing into Marcus's eyes.

"Well, you're right; you are so alike and adorable it was difficult to choose. I don't know really. Just something, just a feeling I can't explain."

"It's cool; I understand," said Hannah.

"What's she up to tonight?" asked Marcus, unable to resist bringing Emma into the conversation at any opportunity.

"Oh, just staying in watching television."

As the evening moved on, Marcus and Hannah learnt more about each other's lives, both choosing the creamy avocado and asparagus pasta for their mains, followed by melting chocolate bombs.

They agreed to meet again. Marcus however, having thoroughly enjoyed his time with Hannah, couldn't wait to see Emma. A few days later he called her mobile.

"Hi, Emma, Marcus here."

"Oh, Hi Marcus, how are you? What can I do for you?"

"I hope you don't mind me calling you. To be frank, I was wondering if you would like to have dinner with me? I've just taken Hannah out, as I'm sure you know, and it was great. I just thought it would be fun to take you to dinner as well, if you don't mind, and if Hannah doesn't mind?"

"Um, well, okay," said Emma, keeping calm and hiding her excitement. "Actually, Hannah's at a conference, returning tomorrow. I could make it tonight?"

"Perfect."

They met at Five Yard, this time oysters, salmon, and figs the main menu choices. Marcus had a wonderful evening, now finding himself enamoured with Emma. For some reason he felt a greater attraction to her than to Hannah. More connection. They continued dating, Hannah not minding in the least. They were both used to this, always happy for each other. By the end of the summer their relationship had become more serious, Emma occasionally staying over at Marcus's apartment, though never exceeding two successive nights. As time moved on, it became increasingly clear that Marcus's priorities remained focused on himself.

"How long will you be away?" asked Emma.

"A couple of days. The flight leaves at eleven on Friday and lands back at Heathrow on Sunday evening."

"This is your third solo trip in two months. I'm not happy, Marcus."

"Emma, we've talked about this. It's the way I am. You said you'd be fine about it."

"I know, but I didn't realise your 'time to yourself' would be so frequent. Drives on your own in the Porsche, dinner alone once a week, trips abroad. I think it's all getting a little too much. I thought we were *together* now."

"Emma, I've explained. I am who I am. I've been totally honest from the start."

"It's too extreme Marcus. It's all about you all the time. That's not how couples exist. They do things together."

"Emma, we *do* do things together; it's just that you want more. Look, I'm not going to change. This is me. I'm perfectly happy with our relationship. I thought you were."

"What you want is an independent life within a relationship. It doesn't work Marcus."

"Emma…"

"No Marcus, I don't want to hear any more. I've had enough. It's over."

Although initially shocked by Emma's outburst and decision to end the relationship, Marcus comfortably fell back into the total solo existence, pursuing his own interests and leisure pursuits. He loved to keep a journal, constantly reviewing his life, reflecting on his achievements, and updating his goals, asking himself every day how he felt and what elements needed to be addressed. He looked after himself, eating the right foods and exercising every day, certainly never worrying about it. He was happy with his body, which he had looked after throughout his life, keeping trim, looking good in whatever clothes he bought - polo shirt and trousers, suit and tie, jumper and jeans, flip flops, shoes, trainers. He could easily have been a model.

Two months after Emma's departure from his life, he was seated in a busy pavement café amongst the magnificent architectural buildings in Prague's Old Town Square, his latest reward to himself for successfully concluding a project with Johnson Worldwide Holdings. His bonus was extremely generous and a three-day trip to Prague, one of his favourite European cities, was first on the list for his next foreign excursion. He ordered two flat whites, one to drink quickly to satisfy his immediate desire for the first coffee of the day, and one extra hot, to drink at a leisurely pace, when two women appeared at his table.

"Excuse me, sorry to disturb you." Marcus looked up. His eyes widened. "I wonder if you wouldn't mind sharing your table. We can't find anywhere else to sit."

He didn't hesitate. "Yes, of course. No problem. Do sit down. There's plenty of room here."

"Thank you. Much appreciated." The women sat down, side by side, taking a position opposite Marcus, once again impressed by the vision before his eyes. Playing it cool, he continued reading his book while they ordered two espressos and a round of rye bread with butter. Very quickly a conversation developed between the three of them, the women revealing they were twins.

"No, really, I would never have thought it. You don't look alike," said Marcus, "though now that you say that, I can see a similarity in the eyes. By the way I'm Marcus." He held out his hand.

"Hello Marcus, nice to meet you. I'm Lauren."

"And I'm Simone."

"Do you feel you have an extra special bond being twins?" asked Marcus, immediately engaged in the topic following his recent experience.

"I don't think so," replied Lauren. "As far as we can work out, we aren't much different from any other sisters other than we share the same birthday, which is quite fun. In fact, that's why we're here; we're celebrating our thirtieth."

"I see. What a great place to come to. Have you been to Prague before?"

"No, this is our first time. How about you?" asked Simone.

"Yes, I've been here quite a few times."

"Ah, you must know the restaurants well then. Where would you recommend?" asked Simone.

"Well, there's the… I tell you what, I've booked La Degustation Bohême Bourgeoise for tonight. It's the best restaurant in town. Michelin starred. Why don't you both join me?"

"No, don't be silly, we couldn't do that, wouldn't be able to afford it. We were looking for something a bit cheaper," said Lauren.

"No problem. My treat."

"What? No, we couldn't possibly…"

"No, I insist. It's your birthdays!"

"Are you sure?"

"Absolutely."

"Okay, why not. We accept."

Marcus and the twins met that night. They both had a good sense of humour, indicating a relaxed and easy-going approach to life; they were intelligent, good conversationalists, and showed signs that they were interested in him, complimenting him on his choice of clothes and the sparkle in his eyes every time he smiled. He was already mulling over in his mind which one he'd like to ask to dinner. Perhaps Lauren had the slight edge appearing slightly more confident and therefore less needy in relationships, considering what had happened with Emma. That night he made his decision. Lauren. They were both from London, so a date was agreed on her return to the city.

The chosen restaurant was Maison La Rouge. Marcus sat at the bar having ordered a dry Martini in anticipation of Lauren's arrival. Ten minutes later she appeared entering through the huge revolving doors, looking a picture of sophistication in her iconic little black dress, six-inch-high heels, and over-the-shoulder full grain leather bag suspended by an elegant gold chain strap. After a second Martini and a glass of dry white wine, they took their seats at the table, Marcus totally enraptured by her confidence, humour and most importantly, her interest in him. However, he couldn't resist bringing her sister into the conversation.

"What's Simone up to tonight then Lauren?"

"Well, she bumped into an old friend at the airport, so they arranged to meet; they've gone to The Gloucester."

"Good choice. An old school chum?" asked Marcus, fishing for more information.

"No, it was her old boss actually. They always got on very well. He was sorry to lose her, but it was time for her to move on."

After an enjoyable time in each other's company, they agreed to meet again.

Despite his wonderment for Lauren, Marcus couldn't stop thinking about Simone. He was most curious as to how Simone would compare with Lauren and couldn't wait to find out. With Lauren unexpectedly having to go away before their second date, he invited Simone out to dinner, as friends of course, and she was happy to agree. Just as it was with Lauren, he had a fantastic time and concluded that both women were as lovely as each other. Confident in the fact that they both liked him, he would have to make a choice. Simone appeared to have the edge; he felt more like himself in her company. Within a couple of months, they were a serious couple, and against the grain of his independent living philosophy, he had asked her to live with him, though not in his own apartment, but in a rented flat. Keeping his apartment, he believed, ensured he would retain his individual identity.

At first, their relationship flourished, but gradually, over time, Simone became increasingly unhappy as Marcus continued to prioritise himself.

"So, Marcus, that was a fantastic achievement, getting that contract with such a lucrative company. What shall we do to celebrate?"

"Well, actually Simone, I've booked a men's spa day at the Park Lane Hotel."

"Really. What does that entail?" asked Simone, her expression of joyful anticipation transforming into puzzled annoyance.

Marcus was unfazed. "All day access to the luxury heated pool, a fifty-minute sports massage, a men's personal facial, an executive foot treatment and a fine dining experience in the hotel's two-star Michelin restaurant. We could go out next week though. I can book a table at The Café Royal. How about next Saturday night?"

"You have got to be kidding. Why can't we celebrate together straight away? Why do you have to do your own thing first?" asked Simone, holding back the tears.

"Simone, we've talked about this. It's the way I am. You said you'd be fine about it."

"What? This is absurd. You've just come back from a week in Amsterdam and now you're going to swan off to The Park Lane Hotel to spoil yourself. How '*fine*' do you want me to be?"

"Look Simone, this is me, I've never pretended to be anyone else. I'm not going to change. I just like being on my own. Being me. Why is that so bad?"

"Because I'm excluded from your life too much Marcus. It's imbalanced. These rewards you give yourself, for your '*personal and business achievements*'; it's ridiculous."

"It may be ridiculous to you but it's important to me. That's how I function. That's how I've got to where I am."

Things didn't change. Marcus continued to prioritise work celebrations and personal successes over joint celebrations with Simone. To reward himself for getting his golf handicap down to sixteen, he took himself off on a two-day trip to Munich Oktoberfest to sample the many fine beers; Löuenbräu, Spatenbräu and Paulaner his favourites, individually tapped from wooden kegs rather than the stainless-steel vats used by other tents, and the wide variety of traditional foods: Wurst, Schweinebraten and Knodel. He loved these festivals. He had attended a couple before but not for a few years. Although a solo attendee, the nature of the festivals offered ample opportunity to meet with people should he choose to. The occasions were always such fun. He loved the splendour of the traditional costumes: women in their dirndls, men in their lederhosen.

He entered the giant tent and took his seat at the long wooden benched table. A couple had already occupied one end, so he sat at the opposite end not wishing to invade their space. They were dressed for the occasion: the man wearing a brown Fedora hat with black and yellow feathers, the woman in blonde pigtails. Definitely a wig, thought Marcus, as he could just make out a dark hairline at the top of her forehead; she hadn't quite pulled it far enough forward. The beer girl arrived in her tight-fitting bodice, high waisted skirt, and white apron. Marcus ordered his drink.

"Paulaner, please. One stein." The single gigantic glass would contain sufficient beer for both his initial thirst-quenching gulps and the subsequent period of unhurried drinking. Marcus sat in total enjoyment, absorbing the atmosphere of the massive marquee, colourful costumes, and melodic melodies of the oompah band's accordion, trumpet and trombone. After ten minutes, following a few glances and friendly nods and smiles, his attention was drawn to a male voice calling out to him from the other end of the table.

"Excuse me Sir, English?"

"Yes."

"I hope you don't mind me asking but would you like to join us?"

Marcus glanced over at the pretty pigtail lady. "Yes, why not? I'd love to," replied Marcus, rising from his seat, stein in hand.

"I'm Leon," said the man, shaking Marcus's hand, "and this is my sister Lilly."

"How do you do? I'm Marcus."

"Nice to meet you," said Lilly.

"We're twins," said Leon, "but you'd never guess. Not an ounce of similarity."

"No, you're right. I'd never have guessed."

Leon and Lilly were both Munich locals and often made trips to the UK on family business. They were also keen golfers and loved to travel around Europe playing on the best golf courses. Conversation flowed naturally, the three of them developing a good rapport. After much drinking and talking, it was time to go their separate ways.

"You must get in touch when you are next in the UK," Marcus insisted.

"Sure, we'd love too. In fact, we're aiming to come over in a couple of weeks," Leon replied.

"Great. Give me a call."

Simone felt increasingly ostracised from life with Marcus but tried her best to show patience, tolerance and understanding. Marcus was fully aware of her dissatisfaction.

"I know you must be really frustrated with me Simone, but we have talked about this. Look, I've got a couple of friends coming over next week who I met in Munich. Let's invite them to dinner." Dining at home as couples wasn't really Marcus's cup of tea, but he did occasionally concede to taking part in activities that didn't interest him to keep his girlfriends happy: taking Emma to La Bohème, even though he hated opera, and although not too keen on cold weather holidays, Simone to Chamonix for a week's skiing. He would reject requests to partake in activities that he was genuinely not prepared to tolerate whatsoever, such as spending a few days away with his girlfriends' parents or joint shopping trips in the local mall. These activities certainly didn't fit in with his philosophy of living the best life he can. At least with the operas and skiing there was an element of self-improvement but time with parents and following his girlfriend around department stores was not part of his agenda.

"Well, this is a departure, Marcus. Okay, that will be nice."

Simone had gone to great lengths to create a welcoming atmosphere for Lilly and Leon, setting out a beautiful dining table with her best crockery and cutlery, and cooking a delicious meal. On their arrival, Marcus was reminded of why he liked this couple so much. Leon was relaxed, fun and loved to live life to the full, and more importantly always demonstrating interest and curiosity in Marcus's life, nourishing him with positive energy and passion. In addition to her beauty, Lilly was also instantly likeable, emitting a similar vibe to Leon, awakening in Marcus feelings he'd never previously experienced. Her eyes always appeared to lock on to him, pupils widening, which in his mind was an invitation to her inner world. In accord with her congenial nature, she was equally attentive to Simone.

"This is lovely Simone, you must give me the recipe," said Lilly.

"To be honest, I just found it on YouTube. I'll send you the link."

"You'll have to come over to Munich. Have you ever been?" asked Lilly.

"No, I haven't. Thanks. That would be great," replied Simone.

"Fantastic, I'll organise it," said Lilly excitedly.

"Can't wait for the golf tomorrow, Leon," said Marcus, quickly moving the conversation on. "Are you ready for defeat?"

Leon grinned. "Don't be too sure now Marcus; our handicaps aren't that far apart."

"Only kidding. It'll be a good day. You'll like the golf club. Great course, good food and fine wine."

"I'm looking forward to it," said Leon.

"Well, we'll have a great time shopping won't we Simone," said Lilly taking hold of Simone's hand across the table, Simone surprised by a fluttery feeling in her stomach.

"I hope so. I'm sorry I'm not a golfer and denying you the opportunity of a foursome."

"No, don't be silly. It's fine," replied Lilly reassuringly, gently squeezing Simone's hand. "It'll be good fun. I can play golf with Leon any time."

Lilly and Leon returned to Munich. Simone thought that this may have been a turning point in her life with Marcus but within a few days all was back to normal, Marcus continuing to spend time alone. Gradually Simone became increasingly worn down with the whole process and couldn't take any more. Within two months she had moved out of the rented flat and Marcus was back in his own apartment.

Marcus was in no way unhappy about losing the two women in his life whom he had fallen in love with or more to the point, thought he had fallen in love with. He continued to have fun, set himself small goals and reward himself when he achieved them. A return to one-night stands and time with friends suited him perfectly, maintaining friendships with Leon and Lilly, and in the autumn he received a call from Leon inviting him over. He didn't hesitate to take up the opportunity of seeing Lilly again. Within days of being in her company, he was hooked, and it wasn't long before he asked her to dinner.

"You mean without Leon, just me?"

"Yes, I would like that very much. Of course, I think Leon is a great guy, but the bottom line is I like you and would like to spend more time with you alone, get to know you on a different level."

"Okay," said Lilly looking directly into his eyes. "When and where have you got in mind? We're going to Zurich in a week."

"How about this Friday? We'll go to La Maison de

Terre."

"Okay."

"Perfect."

Marcus loved Lilly's company and they met again after her trip to Zurich. He made repeated trips between London and Munich to spend time with her. He was now in love with her. By the following spring they were married and moved into a rented house in Kensington. Marcus, ensuring rules were established early on in their relationship, had of course made it clear to Lilly what he was like and that he would need time to himself, maybe a trip abroad or a solo weekend away. Lilly had understood perfectly. She agreed that a healthy relationship involved allowing partners time to themselves to pursue their own interests. Personal freedom, she believed, generates new ideas and activities, which add to relationships, keeping them exciting and engaging.

"So, when's the Madrid trip Marcus?" asked Lilly. "You said you'd be going in a few weeks. That was two months ago."

"It's funny you should ask that now Lilly. I have literally just booked. I'm flying out on Thursday. Back on Sunday."

"Okay. Good. I'm sure you'll have a great time," said Lilly wrapping her arms around him.

"Thanks. I'm sure I will."

Following Marcus's arrival in Madrid, he headed directly for the Westin Palace Hotel, straight to the bar, had a wonderful dinner, treating himself to traditional roast shoulder of milk-fed lamb, ratte potatoes and spring onion, and retired to bed. That night, unusually, he had found it difficult to sleep. He couldn't help thinking about Lilly and lay awake for hours. This was the first night he had been away from her since the wedding.

His next day began with a visit to the Prado Museum and then a lunch booked in Los Montes de Gallacia, but he just couldn't get Lilly out of his mind. He wanted to be with her. He wanted to go home. He aborted his trip and booked a flight back to London to surprise his wife.

As he approached the driveway, the exterior security lights lit up welcoming him home. Entering the front door, he switched on the hall lights and crept upstairs. He approached the bedroom, expecting his wife to be in bed, but as he gently opened the door and peered into the room, lit only by the light of the landing, all he could make out was a made-up bed. Looking around the house, it became obvious there was no one in. He immediately tapped Lilly's name on his phone and awaited her response. His heart was racing.

"Hello Marcus."

"Lilly, where are you?"

"Oh, I'm in Brighton visiting a friend. Why?"

"I'm in the house."

"What? Aren't you meant to be in Madrid? You're not due back for a couple of days yet."

"I know, but I came home early. I missed you."

"Marcus, no, this isn't you. I don't believe it," said Lilly in a slightly humorous manner.

"No seriously, I've missed you. Can't you come home?"

"Yes, of course, but we've arranged to visit the museum in the morning. I'll catch the one o'clock."

"Okay, I suppose I'll have to wait then."

"Marcus, you'll be fine. I'll be back before you know

it."

"Okay, see you tomorrow then. Love you."

"Ich liebe dich auch."

"What does Marcus want this time of night?" asked Simone, pulling over the duvet for Lilly's return.

"Says he's come home early because he's missing me."

"Well, that's a first. You must have something particularly special."

"Oh, believe me, I have. Now where were we?"

The following morning Marcus headed out for his morning coffee, eagerly excited in anticipation of Lilly's arrival, and plenty of time before his lunchtime appointment at his local estate agents. The market was up; he'd get a good price. Placing his newspaper on the table, he raised his hand to grab the waiter's attention.

"Good morning, sir, what can I get you?"

"Good morning. A flat white please?"

"Yes sir. Will there be anything else?"

"No thank you."

"Certainly sir."

SNATCH

They all loved Micaela. They looked up to her. She was cool. Because she stole things. During break times the kids would gather round her like excited punters eager to make a quick profit in the financial markets. There was always something for somebody: lipsticks, cigarettes, nail varnish. If they wanted something Micaela could get it, the primary source for goods being the local indoor market.

Micaela was tall for a fourteen-year-old; five and a half feet with shoulder-length brown hair parted at the centre. Lots of it. Thick. Wavy. Stormy. When not in school uniform, and out in town for weekend goodie gathering, she would make sure she didn't appear like a member of the Saturday morning wild-teen hunting pack displaying a rapacious appetite to cause mayhem wherever they appeared. No, she'd be stripped of these personality layers and go solo. Far more fruitful. Hair tied back, casual blue jeans, loose knitted jumper, smart white trainers. She was good at her craft, trained by her mother: the less you stick out the better; always have a large purse with a snap button closure with you that can stand up on its own; stay calm and non-threatening; wander and browse confidently and casually. No, not for her the wolf, but the hawk. Ready to swoop. The target object in her bag in seconds.

At eighteen she attended university. Of course, there was never any shortage of candy in whatever shape or form for her and her flatmates: chocolate, wine, gin, eyeliner, mascara, socks. At first there was disapproval and concern about this woman who styled herself as a pocketful of possibilities. But the temptation was too much. They signed up to it, becoming used to the treats, and ultimately accepting them as normality - cheese and wine - a natural extension of their student loans. She studied religion, having always been fascinated by human existence and purpose. Not that she was particularly religious herself. And in no way were there any religious beliefs in the family. That box was empty. But she did find religious studies interesting, fascinated by the range of beliefs as to why we are here, what we do while we are here, and what happens after we are here. In her mind she'd preside in each chair extolling the virtues of each creed, and be the debating audience – challenging, arguing, disputing. The Five Pillars. Rebirth. Jesus is the son of God. The resurrection. The soul is God-given and immortal.

At twenty-one it was time to get a job. She'd gained a 2.1 in Theology, though it was never her aim to pursue a religious career. It was just that she knew the subject like a viper knows its venom. She had full confidence in the fact that this outer garment would stand her in good stead amidst turbulent thoughts of what to do in life. Her main aim was always to obtain the degree and take it from there. She wasn't ready for commitment. Not ready to expose her physical being to the stresses and strains of career-based employment and the endless pursuit of stepping on to the escalator to convey her to the next level. For the time being any job would do.

The Red Lion was a busy city centre pub, a former bank, run by Alison Carmichael. A huge place. Three levels: main ground floor bar, lower ground floor for party bookings, and mezzanine floor for those who like to look down on others. Micaela was happy to frame herself within this disordered fabric of city society: from lives gifted with rich fibres to those stained with decay and neglect. Micaela had gradually increased her responsibilities by working in the kitchen, collecting dead glasses from the tables, waitressing, and now working behind the bar. She'd got to know the pub inside out, ready to swoop at the slightest opportunity for hats, scarves, shopping bags, credit cards. No pin needed these days; tap and purchase before their absence is noticed, then dispose of them straight away. Most likely people are so drunk that when morning arrives, they won't know they have lost anything or bother to retrace their steps to find them again. Micaela knew this only too well, circling, scouting her prey, spotting the most vulnerable groups. Her room in her shared flat was a store of delight.

She admired her boss. Kind, considerate, brave. Well, they say opposites attract. Alison had donated a kidney to her sister Sophie three years earlier enabling her to live a normal, healthy life.

"Good morning, Micaela. How are you today?"

"Yes, great thanks. How about you? How was your day off?"

"Yes, good. Muscles aching this morning though." Alison stooped down to massage the backs of her calves. "Ran 10K yesterday."

"Oh, I didn't know you were a runner. You've never said anything."

"Oh, didn't I? Yes, I belong to a running club. Got a half-marathon coming up soon. Raising money for charity. That will be a challenge."

"Wow, that's great. God, I wouldn't last half a mile."

"Oh, you get used to it once you've built up the initial strength and stamina. You should try it."

"Maybe one day," replied Micaela making her way into the main bar. "I see the cleaner's been in. I'll get the chairs down."

"Thanks Micaela. I'll see to the admin." Alison opened her laptop to check the day's deliveries.

"Oh, by the way, how's your mum?" asked Micaela.

"Usual. One minute she knows me, the other she doesn't. I think she's getting worse. The decline is becoming more rapid. It's been a year now. I visit her every day, but the truth is I'm gradually becoming a stranger."

At eleven thirty they had completed their preparations for the first customers of the day and sat down for a cup of coffee, a rare opportunity for a good chat.

"So, you studied theology at university. That must have been interesting," Alison remarked as she wrapped both hands around her favourite mug: *Coffee Warms the Soul*.

"Yes fascinating. It's always interested me. The odd thing is that I'm not at all religious myself. My parents certainly never passed on any particular belief. My father left when I was three. Off with another woman. We didn't have any money. It was a struggle. My mother coping on her own. And she certainly didn't demonstrate any models of moral code. Too busy with boyfriends, cigarettes, and booze."

"No brothers or sisters?"

"Nope. Just me. I used to get out of the house as much as I could. My aunt worked in the local library, and I used to get dumped there for hours. And that's how I got into religion. There were the usual kiddie books, but I was always fascinated by the front covers of the religious books. They were always weird and colourful, with elephants or monkeys or cows, and characters with eight arms. Of course, as I grew older, I would read them. It was an eye opener. Coming from no knowledge whatsoever of different beliefs about life and where we come from, what I was reading seemed crazy, but fascinating. Dying and coming back as a rabbit?"

"So, nothing you read offered any specific direction for you?"

"No. Difficult when you haven't any family background to grow your beliefs from. Even after university I'm still open about the whole thing. How about you? Well, obviously Christian?"

"Yes. Through and through. And yes, you're right, it's because of my parents. They were church goers and with such a strong belief in the family, you just become what they are. Of course, you have a choice as you become an adult and can reject or accept what you've grown up with. For me it is acceptance and I try and live my life along Christian morals and beliefs. Quite simply to love God and to love others."

"And eternal life in Heaven," interjected Micaela. "The soul will live on past the death of the physical body."

"Yes," nodded Alison.

"As long as you believe in Christ and have led a good life."

"God will be the judge."

"Otherwise, it's Hell?"

"I'm afraid so," said Alison. "If you reject God and commit sins, you will go to hell for the rest of eternity."

"What do you make of other beliefs?" asked Micaela. "Reincarnation. Staying in your grave until the day of judgement."

"I respect other beliefs. God has given free will. But for me it's Christianity. My soul will go to heaven," she affirmed, finishing her drink before standing up to return the mug to the sink. She looked at the clock; the minute hand was approaching the twelve. "Come on. The first customers will be in any minute now. Let's get cracking!"

Following another profitable weekend of masterful misappropriation, Micaela arrived for work, bang on time. She had already learnt from Alison the power of punctuality. It shows, she had said, that you are organised and dependable and that you respect your co-workers. They in turn respect you. She removed her leather jacket, hung it on the coat rack and proceeded to the bar to begin her duties. Alison had already noticed when Micaela walked in that the jacket looked familiar. Mainly because of its dark green colour rather than the usual black, and the fact that several weeks ago she had personally dashed out after a customer to return it after she had left it over the back of a chair. Alison had remembered liking the jacket with its distinctive angled gold zip pockets mid-way up each side, giving it an edge, as if the jacket itself will hold you in contempt if you express even a hint of dislike for the design. She thought no more of it.

Later that morning she received a phone call.

"Oh, hi, I was just wondering if you had found a green leather jacket, or if anybody has handed one in. I was wearing it on Friday night and left the pub without it. I didn't ring the next day because I've been unwell and stuck in bed all weekend. It was only when I was getting ready to go to work this morning that I couldn't find it. The only thing I could think of is that I left it in your pub as that's the last place I've been to."

"Oh, um, I don't think so. Just a minute, I'll have a look."

"Thanks."

Alison stood silently for a minute and then returned to the call.

"No, can't see it anywhere. Sorry."

"Oh, Okay. Well, look, if anyone hands one in, please can you give me a ring?"

"Of course, I will. I'm sorry I couldn't help you. Good luck."

"Thanks. Bye."

"Bye."

Alison ended the call and immediately located Micaela's jacket. She removed it from the coat rail and inspected it. Surely, not Micaela. It was time for a chat. Micaela was preparing the main bar for customers.

"Micaela, have you got a minute?"

"Yes, sure."

"Can you come through to the back?" asked Alison politely, leading the way to the kitchen.

Micaela followed.

"Yes, of course. Everything alright?"

"Please, sit down Micaela, I just want to ask you something."

"Sure." They sat at the kitchen table facing each other. "What is it?"

"Look," said Alison staring directly into Micaela's eyes, "forgive me for asking this but a customer has just rung in asking if she'd left her jacket behind."

"Oh, okay."

"A green leather jacket," added Alison, her gaze still fixed on Micaela.

Micaela's heart picked up pace. "Okay."

"Like the one hanging on the coat rail."

"Oh, yes, like mine. That's a coincidence."

"Is it?"

"Well yes. Alison, surely you don't think I took it."

"Micaela, Listen. Just tell me the truth. She left it on Friday; you were here. And as soon as you walked through the door this morning, I recognised the jacket. I'd rescued it for the same customer some weeks ago. I remember it because of its gold zip pockets and I really liked it. It's the same jacket. Don't be afraid to tell me the truth."

"Honestly Alison, it's mine. I bought it at the weekend."

"Micaela," said Alison firmly, certain that Micaela was lying.

Micaela sensed her face flood with blood. No longer the predator; now the prey. She had never been caught in all these years. She was normally so skilful at diverting suspicion away from her. An expert in her art. How on earth did she slip up? It's obvious that it's the jacket. She'll have to own up. She has too much respect for Alison. She looks up to Alison. The best form of defence in this case will be to acquiesce and not fight back.

"God, Alison, I'm so sorry. Yes, it was me. I'm sorry." Micaela dropped her head and covered her face with her hands.

Alison furrowed her eyebrows. "Micaela. How could you? What on earth possessed you to do such a thing?"

Micaela reappeared from behind her mask. "I don't know. I am so sorry. I'd collected it with all the other stuff left behind, took it to the back and just as I was about to go home, I just couldn't resist it. It was lovely. I thought, nobody's going to know. It was wrong of me, I'm so sorry."

"Micaela, listen. I must ask you this. Have you taken anything else since you've started working here? Bags, wallets, phones?"

"No, honestly, it's just that I couldn't resist the jacket. It's not me. It was a moment of madness. I don't understand it myself. I'm so sorry." Tears flowed down Micaela's red cheeks, human fluids dominating her dispirited countenance. "Are you going to report me to the police? I understand if you fire me but please don't report me to the police."

"Well, that depends, Micaela. What you've done is shocking. I'm completely taken aback. You've come here to work and are doing a great job. And then this, out of the blue."

"No, honestly Alison. I don't understand it myself. Maybe I need to see someone."

"Look, this is what we are going to do. I will ring the customer back. Tell her that the jacket was here all the time, lost under a pile of clothing, and simply return it. She will be so grateful; she won't pursue it any further. And yes, go and see someone."

Micaela's eyes widened. "Are you sure?"

"Yes. Deep down, and from what I know about you, this isn't typical. We all deviate now and again. None of us is perfect. And I'm sure you won't do anything like this again. Will you?"

"No, of course not. You mean you're not going to sack me?"

"No, I'm going to give you the benefit of the doubt. That this is a one off. To be quite honest, I don't want to lose you."

"God Alison, thank you so much. I promise. Nothing like this will ever happen again."

"Good, now let's get back to work."

The following weekend Micaela reflected on the week's events. How could she have been so careless? All these years with getting away with it. Well, in truth she had got away with it. She'd been forgiven, and she still has a job. It could easily have gone the other way, and the police being involved. Maybe it's time to turn over a new leaf. Leave the stealing behind. Look at Alison. What a wonderful woman. Why can't she be more like her? That night she dreams:

She is at the pub. Alison is late. Micaela confronts her.

"Alison. I don't understand. Every morning you are late. This isn't like you. And where did you get that jacket from?"

"Oh, I found it in a coffee shop on Sunday morning."

"Sunday morning? Weren't you running?"

"No, I've given that up. Too early. Can't be bothered anymore."

"That's a shame Alison. You were doing such a great job."

Micaela is now visiting a care home.

"Hello Mrs Carmichael. I'm Micaela. Sorry Alison can't come today. She's gone to a movie."

"Who? Alison? I've never heard of her."

"I've brought you some flowers. Roses. I hope you like them."

"Oh, thank you so much, that's very kind of you."

Micaela is outside a charity shop. She arrives promptly for her volunteering work. She carries in the black bags of clothing left outside the shop and tips them out all over the floor. She's now back in the pub. Alison's jacket is hanging on the coat rack, pockets stuffed with wallets, credit cards and smart phones. Micaela walks in. "Oh my God. Where did all that come from? Alison, what have you been doing? Sit down. We need to talk."

"Are you going to sack me?"

"Alison. You know me better than that. Of course not. This isn't you. I'll make sure everything is returned to their rightful owners and you can have a fresh start."

Thank you, Micaela. Thank you so much. It will never happen again."

The scene switches to a police station. Alison, bereft of human spirit, is dragging Micaela through the entrance doors, THIEF scrawled across Micaela's forehead in red lipstick. 'I want to report a crime.'

Micaela wakes up. Or she thinks she does. Sticky. Clammy. She feels something heavy resting on her feet. She sits up. There is nothing there. A white dove circles the ceiling.

Micaela, weary from her restless night, arrived for work only to discover the entrance door locked. Using her own set of keys, she entered the building. As she closed the door behind her, her phone rang.

"Hello."

"Hello Micaela."

"Hi Sophie. How's things?"

"Um, well, not too good. I'm afraid I've got some very bad news."

"Oh no. What?"

"Brace yourself; it's Alison."

"What?"

"She's dead."

Micaela freezes. "What?" How?"

"She collapsed during her half-marathon yesterday."

"Oh my God. I can't believe it. That's terrible. I'm so sorry. What was it? A heart attack?"

"We don't know anything for sure yet. We'll know more in due course. They managed to get her to hospital but unfortunately there was nothing more they could do. She died in the early hours."

"I'm so sorry Sophie. You must be devastated."

"Thank you. You must be too."

"Yes, I am. It's unbelievable. She was such a fantastic lady. She'd do anything for anybody, as you know. I couldn't have asked for a better boss."

"I can give you a call later and update you on what's happening. In the meantime, are you okay for opening up? If not, I understand. I've arranged for a relief manager. He should be there in an hour."

"Yes, of course, I'm already in. That's fine."

"Thanks so much. I'll give you a call later."

"That will be good. Thank you. And once again I'm so sorry Sophie."

"Thank you. Speak later then."

"Okay, Bye."

"Bye."

Shocked and dazed, Micaela set about her usual routines; life goes on: sweep the floor, take down the chairs, rinse the pumps, check the barrels. Opening the cellar door, she pushed down the light switch, took hold of the handrail, and stepped onto the concrete staircase, still deep in shock thinking about Alison. As she did so, the strip-lights flickered and flashed, normally a sign of coming to life, but in this case demise, returning the cellar to semi-darkness, the only light source now coming from the open door. She took a further few steps when her phone signalled a text. She removed her hand from the handrail, paused, and read the message: *Shouldn't be long. Fifteen mins. Bill. Relief Manager.* Continuing down the stairs using both thumbs to make a brief reply, she placed her right foot too far over the edge of the next step causing her to lose her balance. Before she knew it, she tumbled down the steps hitting her head several times. Within seconds she was sprawled out on the cellar floor unconscious.

Sophie couldn't believe that she was making a second visit to Whittingsdale Hospital in such a short period of time. Same intensive care unit, same seat. She had been told Micaela will not pull through. She was in her final moments of human existence, unable to open her eyes or move any part of her body. The muscles surrounding her mouth twitched involuntarily, suggesting a momentary smile. She breathed in sharply, paused, and from deep within her lungs, exhaled her final breath.

Sophie sat in silence, gazing at Micaela's lifeless body, just as she had with Alison's. Behind her, a robin appeared at the window, at first standing motionless and erect, then, after making a series of short runs and hops, cocked its head, thrust its bill towards the vulnerable worm, snatched it up, and flew away.

ABOUT THE AUTHOR

David Evans is a former headteacher, university tutor, and accredited life coach. Previous books include, *Depicted: Eight Short Stories of Life's Dilemmas, Mysteries and Surprises*, and *Talking About Henry: a guide to achieving your goals and dreams*. David also writes music and is the composer of the album, *Henry VIII and His Six Wives: A Contemporary Soundtrack*. This was performed in The National Portrait Gallery. His most recent musical project, *Love Design and Destiny,* poems and songs about love's ups and downs, was performed in London's Soho. He has featured on *LA Talk Radio* discussing his writing and composing and has contributed to Writing Magazine's *Writers Online* advice column: *Follow Your Creative Calling.*